I0713967

First edition independently printed 2023.
This edition printed 2024 by Pope Lick Press.

DEREK HEATH

DROP BEAR

OUTBACK TERROR
BOOK ONE

HOPE LICK PRESS
2024

PROLOGUE
US AND THE SKINKS

The desert sun was fading, fat tendrils of heat banking into the clouds as it pulsed in a desperate attempt to remain ignited. The red yolk of the sky bled onto the ground down the silhouettes of peaks on the horizon; sand shifted lazily over the dry, cracked surface of a vast and largely empty plain. The crusts of trees, their branches gnarled and barren, exploded from that surface like splintered, stubby fingers.

A dim firelight glimmered at the base of a thick pillar of smoke, three dark shapes hunched over the flame. Small boulders and rocks were scattered around them, backpacks laid on the sand beside a pair of hastily-erected canvas tents. A tall boab tree behind the tents cast a thick wedge of shadow over them, not with its sparse canopy but its titanic, barrel-like trunk.

"I haven't been this far from Willowra since I was in Venturers," one of the figures said drunkenly, thick knots of glowing, red hair framing eyes that glinted sharply in the firelight. Michelle's legs were bare, her knees drawn up to her chest, and she gripped a half-empty bottle of Bundaberg by the neck, swinging it softly against her thigh. "I thought Petey Camber was going to have his way with me."

"Petey Camber from high school?" giggled the young woman sitting next to her on the rock. "I can't believe you and Petey got it on at *Venturers*, of all things."

"Hey, I said I *thought* he was going to."

"He didn't?"

"He was a coward," the first woman grinned. She tipped back the bottle and drank a little before offering it to the second. "Everyone else was getting busy in their tents; me and Petey Camber just sat and watched the stars."

"*Bo—ring*," Tanya said, swiping the bottle. She nodded across the fire toward the third member of the little group. He'd been drinking silently for the last half hour. In the encroaching dark, it was hard to tell whether he was even still awake. "What about you, Dylan? You ever get up to much out here?"

The man flashed his teeth in the firelight and took a swig from his own can before setting it down with a bunch of crumpled empties at his feet. He was tall and lanky, even hunched over like he was, and the Darwin Buffaloes cap on his head was tattered and frayed at the visor. The thick scruff of a beard obscured his lower jaw. "Never came out to the desert before I was twenty," he slurred. "Thought a damn *Yowie* was gonna get me."

"A Yowie?" Tanya grinned. "The hell is that, dickhead?"

Michelle elbowed her in the ribs, giggling as she gestured for the bottle back. "Dyl's scared of the Bigfoot," she murmured. "Hey, gimme that."

Tanya was the taller of the two, and her muscular shoulders shone with sweat in the fading dusk-light. She wore Dylan's Buffaloes vest and a pair of combat trousers that were scuffed and sandy. Dark hair, pinned behind her head, erupted in a messy ponytail slung across the back of a tanned neck. "Bigfoot?" she said seriously, turning back to the man across the campfire.

Dylan shrugged. Looking past her into the wilderness, he said, "I was a kid. That shit terrified me. Weren't no Bigfoot, though. Nah. The Yowie's a spirit. Only comes out at night. Monstrous thing." He smiled wickedly, reaching for his can again. "That's what my mam told me, anyway."

"Dyyyl's a-fraid of a Biiiig—foot," Michelle sang, laughing to herself as she took another drink. "Dyyyyyyl… hey, I forget the rest."

Gently, Tanya reached out and clamped her palm

over the bottle's neck, lowering it a little. Michelle didn't seem to notice. She and Dylan had been going steady for four or five years now, and Tanya had been worried that she'd spend most of her time awkwardly third-wheeling if she joined them this weekend, but so far the mood had been relaxed and comfortable. "All right, which is it?" she said. "This Yowie. Is it a Bigfoot or a spirit?"

"It's not real," Dylan said. "It's folklore, you know?"

"Humour me," Tanya rolled her eyes.

Somewhere behind them, something scuffled through the sand. Probably a bustard, Michelle thought, glancing back into the dark. The sunlight was nearly all gone, blossoms of red on the horizon all that remained. She couldn't see anything out there; the sound had stopped.

Fucking birds.

"Okay," Dylan leant forward with the pretence of stoking the fire with a thick hunk of smooth eucalyptus he'd found in the sand a couple miles back. Really, she saw, he was enjoying relaying this nonsense. *Well, let him.* She wasn't quite as cooked as the others, but she was just pissed enough to enjoy a ghost story. "Nobody can say for sure where it came from, or what it's really called – my mam called it the Yowie, but my pop – her dad – always called it the *Yahoo*. They both agreed it was a big nasty fucker. Massive, hairy thing, covered in fur, looked a little like a gorilla I guess—"

"That's Bigfoot!" Michelle hissed, snatching the bottle from Tanya's grip and taking another slug. "You're talking about Bigfoot, you dumb dick!"

From nearby came the faint scratching sounds of something scuttling up the thick trunk of the boab.

Dylan shrugged. "Whatever you want to call it," he offered, shooting Tanya a look. "In NSW they call it the *Ghindaring*. I reckon someone I used to know called it the *Wawee*. Yahoo-Devil Devil. Hairy man of the wood. Point is, whatever it is… it stalks the outback at night. When the moon is full, probably."

"Are you trying to add *colour* to this dumb story?" Tanya giggled.

"Sure, why not." Stretching, Dylan continued. "So in the late eighteen hundreds, one guy claims to see this thing, covered in black hair – kinda coppery around its neck – and throws a rock at it. I guess it scampers off into the bush, because the next thing you know he's calling up the Australian Museum and saying he'll go grab it for them, for a fee. Guess he never did, because thirty-odd years later there's a bunch more sightings. Skip ahead to 1907, a couple's driving to the coast from Braidwood and see a Yowie on the side of the road. Over two metres tall, covered in hair, arms dragging on the ground. Few years ago, some guy in Canberra sees one in his garage. Again – covered in hair, arms almost touching the ground."

There was a pause, and for a moment it seemed that the three of them were considering. The shadows danced briefly as something hopped between the branches of the boab tree behind the tents. Then Tanya said flatly, "That's just Bigfoot, Dylan. Wouldn't you say, Mish?"

"Bigfoot," Michelle agreed.

"Fine," Dylan grunted, hauling himself to his feet and pulling up his khakis. "I need a piss."

"Do it away from the tents," Tanya suggested, leaning over to swipe the bottle again. "Let me have some of this. Thought I was drunk enough for his shit."

"Impossible," Michelle said, gladly handing her the Bundaberg. "Never can be."

"Fair enough." She drank, cringing a little as the rum burned her throat. "Not much of this left, you know. Reckon we'll find somewhere to stop tomorrow and get some more?"

"Pfff," Michelle shrugged. "We're miles away from anywhere. I'm hoping there's another bottle in the trunk."

"Fine. Hey, d'you wanna go set fire to dickhead's thongs?" Tanya said quietly, nodding across the fire to the sandals the man had left in the sand by his rocky perch.

"*Shit* yeah," Michelle said.

"I can hear you!" Dylan yelled from somewhere behind the tents.

"*Shit* yeah," Michelle whispered.

Tanya giggled. "Fucking Yowie." Calling into the dark, she said, "We're gonna burn your thongs if you're not back in twelve seconds, Yowie!"

"Fucking Yowie," Michelle nodded wisely.

"Nothing out here but us and the skinks," Tanya muttered, standing up to stretch in the firelight.

Dylan staggered barefoot away from the fire, the sand still uncomfortably hot but and scratchy but the thought of sliding his soles back into the cracked leather of his thongs proportionately unbearable. He grunted to himself as he swayed past the tents and toward the enormous boab tree, already unbuckling his shorts.

"I'm gonna piss on your tent," he sang happily to himself, but then he looked at the tents and quickly realised that he wasn't sure which was which. The song abruptly ended and he shrugged, resigning himself to the tree.

The trunk of the thing was as wide as a car and about the height of two men stacked together (he imagined the second standing on the first's shoulders). The bark was smooth and the thick roots seemed to punch up into the trunk itself, forming thick grey whorls. Branches shot out from the top of the trunk in all directions, each one exploding into a mess of twisted claws. In the dark, the branches seemed to fuse into a nest of shadow at the centre.

Glancing about furtively, Dylan positioned himself around the back of the tree and dropped his shorts. He could only have drunk five or six cans but the effect on his bladder had been niggling him for an hour or so. Swaying a little, he started to urinate, tipping his head back and looking up into the branches of the boab.

"Fucking Yowie," he murmured. "Dumb story. Thanks, Mam."

Shivering, he narrowed his eyes as the silhouetted claws of the branches above his head seemed to bough and twist together. Just a trick of the moonlight. There was a part of him, however small, that had taken those stories in as a child and never really agreed to dispute them as fiction; a part that, now, told him – quite impossibly – that there was something in the boab.

"Oh, fuck off," he whispered, shaking himself off and reaching for his shorts to heave them back up his bare legs. Looking back toward the tents, he wondered if they'd really do something to his shoes. Probably already had, by now.

Something snapped above his head. The *crunch* was dry and brittle, like breaking bone.

He looked up.

The branches swayed a little, bouncing softly with the weight of something mobile, something fast. Whatever it had been – bustard, bilby, whatever – it was gone now.

Shrugging it off, Dylan started to buckle his shorts.

A shape dropped from the tree and smashed into his back, claws sliding through his shirt and into his skin with a delicate *snick*. Dylan yelled as the sudden weight on his upper body bowled him onto his front in the sand. Spitting out a cloud of red earth and twisting onto his back, he yowled as the thing clamped between his shoulder-blades withdrew itself, climbing onto his chest. Struggling to bat the thing off, Dylan looked up to see a black, hunched shape almost his height, tufted protrusions shooting out of a wide, swinging head. Bright white eyes flashed through clumps of matted fur.

"Get off me!" he yelled. The thing hissed in response, its snout yawing wide open, enormous sharpened molars glinting in the moonlight.

Blood winged from his neck as the creature clamped its jaws shut around his throat and ripped out his windpipe. Dylan convulsed as the thing punched its claws into his shoulders and guzzled hungrily at the raw, spouting hole of his neck. There was a commotion by the campfire as the others realised something was happening; they were too late.

Dylan went still and the creature looked up as two silhouettes appeared behind it, whipping its head around to look in their direction.

Michelle screamed, grabbing for the other woman

as the thing leapt off Dylan's limp body and hissed loudly, its piercing cry echoing across the Tanami Desert as it barrelled through the air.

1
TO TANAMI

The aeroplane ploughed through turgid yellow clouds, heat ripping great banks of shimmering, pinkish haze off the wings as the morning sunlight rode the Boeing's tail. The desert was certainly somewhere below them, but separated from the passengers of the 787-9 Dreamliner with a layer of shine-stained puffy white that looked almost solid enough to walk upon, were one so inclined.

Thus far the flight from London Heathrow had been largely uneventful, though Claire had been tempted several times over the last seventeen hours to request politely of the stewardess that the child kicking the back of her seat be painlessly put to death. For most of the journey she had been listening to The Pines' earliest albums on repeat through her headphones and attempting to let the soft, folksy music send her to sleep; whereas usually this might work, she found that the constantly changing air pressure and the anxiety in her chest wouldn't allow it. She had never been able to sleep on aeroplanes; she didn't mind flying, wasn't perturbed by it as such – in fact, since the death of her parents over a dozen years ago, she had been much less inclined to go anywhere in a Volvo than on a Qantas Dreamliner – but she did find that the semi-noticeable shuddering of the plane put her in a state of alertness that wouldn't abate, no matter what she was listening to.

About an hour ago, anyway, her Bluetooth headphones had died, still clamped to her skull when the robotic voice told her in no uncertain terms that the advertised twenty-four-hour battery life was *not* as reliable as she'd hoped. Removing the headphones, she took the time to discretely survey the passengers around her, imagining that many of them were headed for the desert not because they wished to spend any time down there in the sand but because flights to Granites had been significantly cheaper to Broome or Darwin, and that there'd be a whole fleet of Ubers waiting for them at the airport gates; she liked to think that at least a couple had planned to camp out in the desert, though she'd no desire herself to discover the starry skies and dazzling sunsets of Tanami. Whatever their reasons for being out here, she was certain that most of the Dreamliner's passengers were, at least, here by choice.

If not for Eurydice, she'd never have come out here.

Beside her an overweight man in grey jogging bottoms and a *Judge Dredd* t-shirt was reading a thick Jeff VanderMeer paperback and had made it about thirty pages deeper into the novel since the last time she'd glanced in his direction; across the aisle, a young couple sat holding hands on the armrest and talking quietly about the latest episode of *Married at First Sight* with accents that seemed decidedly Australian to her. Directly behind Claire the child had finally fallen asleep – lucky bastard – offering her back a brief respite from the rhythmic thumps that had assaulted it for most of the journey. The devil-child's mother was sleeping too and snoring loudly.

Looking out the window, Claire could see little of the vast, sandy landscape below save for flashes of orange and burnt ochre through tiny cracks in the cloud layer. The clouds themselves formed a remarkably flat surface, sunlight bouncing off wispy heaps of mist-white to splash the creamy contours with gold. The Boeing trembled a little as it was bounced between flanks of breezy wind. They couldn't have been far now; she hadn't slept for twenty hours and knew that she wouldn't have much of a chance once they landed, but once the interview was done, she planned to—

There was a sudden gasp from the front of the

Dreamliner and she turned her head forward, peering down the aisle as the sound turned to a strangled, gargling wheeze. Beside her the overweight man lowered his book a little, following the direction of her gaze to pinpoint the source of the noise. Claire could hardly see past the seat in front of her but she caught a glimpse of one arm flailing into the aisle, the fingers clutching desperately at air.

"Shit," the overweight man whispered, glancing toward the back of the plane. Across the aisle the young couple were doing the same, apparently looking for any sign that a stewardess had heard the sound. "Is he having a heart attack?"

"Could be," Claire said anxiously, looking up and down the aeroplane. "The flight attendants should know first aid. They can deal with this."

All around her people were starting to cock their heads as the wheezing continued, the man near the front of the Boeing clearly having some kind of attack; voices echoed about the pressure chamber of the aeroplane, some calling for a steward to come and help, others standing in their seats to get a better look at the man. Claire's eyes were laser-focused on the arm hanging over the armrest of the chair, the clutching fingers losing strength as the convulsions slowed. There didn't seem to be any flight attendants around. Shit, she thought. Shit, shit, shit…

"Does anyone here know first aid?" somebody

called, and she squeezed her eyes shut. There it was. The sentence she'd been dreading, the one she'd known was coming. The one she had an answer for. She gave it a moment, hoping that somebody else – anybody else – would answer. Nothing came. The silence hung over every passenger, pregnant and waiting to be burst.

Shit.

"I'm coming," she called, fumbling with her seatbelt.

Beside her the overweight man looked over, surprise flaring in his eyes. "You need me to get up?"

Claire struggled to stand, ignoring him and squeezing out into the aisle, not bothering to apologise as she stamped on what she hoped was his left foot. She could feel the eyes on her back, lasers pinned to her spine from every direction, could hear the murmurs all around her as she stumbled down the aisle, praying that a stewardess would miraculously appear, that some other damn person could do this.

All Claire could think about was Eurydice.

The man had stopped convulsing and lay slumped in his chair, mouth hanging open, eyes rolled up in his head. He must have been in his sixties, his cheeks sallow, eyes sunk into deep wrinkled pits. His combover was thin and shock-white, a thick wet rope of drool hanging off his bottom lip and onto the lapel of a pastel-blue cardigan. Both hands gripped the armrests stiffly, the fingers curled into claws.

Beside him a young woman had clamped her hand over the eyes of a girl that Claire presumed was her daughter. As Claire jabbed the pads of her fingers against the old man's throat she nodded to the woman. "I need a defibrillator," she said calmly. "Go to the back of the plane, see if you can find one. And fetch a stewardess. There must be one somewhere. Check the toilets."

The woman stared at her blankly. The old man's neck was cold and clammy, the arteries flat and indiscernible. No pulse.

"Unresponsive," Claire murmured. Glancing sharply at the woman, she said, *"Now."*

As the woman let go of her child's face and scrambled past her, Claire hooked her hands into the man's elbows and tried to lift him out of the seat. His body was limp but had solidified into a sitting position, making it awkward to get him up. Though the mania had kicked in and was pumping through her like hot iron, he was too heavy. Anxiously Claire glanced across the aisle and her eyes met those of a man in his late thirties, his own hair beginning to thin at the forehead. He was watching wide-eyed, and she realised now that he was the one who'd called for a first aider. His jacket was open to reveal a plain white shirt with coffee stains decorating one breast, a neat flower of brown and black faded into the fabric.

"I need to get him into the aisle," she said. "Help me."

"You know what you're doing?"

She swallowed. Thought of Eurydice again. *Did* she know what she was doing? Would she *be* on this flight if that were true? "I'm a doctor," she said simply. "*Help* me."

Nodding frantically, Coffee Stain surged forward and helped her scoop the elderly man out of his chair. They dropped him awkwardly onto his back in the aisle and Claire straddled him, forced into the less-than-dignified position by the lack of space between the seats. She could feel dozens of pairs of eyes on her as she composed herself, feel blood pumping loudly in her ears. The Boeing shuddered as she knotted her hands together and laid them on the old man's chest. *You're running out of time. Do it.*

She flattened her hands over the old man's scrawny chest, feeling his ribs through the material of his cardigan. Drawing in a sharp breath, she started compressions. Somewhere, somebody screamed as they realised what was happening. Almost everybody was standing in their seats now, rows and rows of heads bobbing up to watch. Somebody was fumbling with their phone to call triple zero. Her hair was in her eyes, thick, dark tangles of it.

There was a dreadful dry *crunch* as she slammed her palms into the old man's chest. She ignored it, kept pumping, counting in her head until she reached thirty. Arms aching she leant forward, tipping his head back and pinching his nose before breathing hard into his airway. She heard the clicking of heels and glanced up to see the stewardess finally coming, but it was too late. Stopping now to hand this over to the woman would only waste precious seconds the unresponsive old geezer didn't have. A silent understanding passed between them and Claire returned to her compressions, praying that the woman from the front row had found a defibrillator, praying that this would work, praying that all the people staring at her right now would somehow miraculously forget her face after this if it didn't.

"Come on," she whispered breathlessly as she pumped the man's fragile chest, ignoring another dry *crack*. "Come on…"

She was leaning forward to breathe into his mouth again when his body convulsed, a thick wet bolt of air shooting up his throat. He sputtered into life and Claire moaned with relief, staggering off him and back into the aisle as the stewardess finally took over. She watched through a haze of vertigo as the uniformed woman laid the old man's head on her lap and smiled down at him. Only now did Claire notice the rheumy nature of the man's eyes, the cyanosis of his lips, the dark stain of his corduroy trousers that meant he'd likely soiled himself.

This was more than just a heart attack.

Somebody clapped her on the back and jolted her out of her shock, ripping her back into the present. "Gee willikers," somebody else said, their voice floating somewhere around the back of her head. "Look at that, you saved the poor bugger."

Claire glanced toward the old man's empty seat. Her heart was still pounding, adrenaline working through her like a bullet train sliding manically between tracks.

"Yeah," she whispered, Eurydice's face flashing in her mind. "Guess I did."

The Qantas 787-9 Dreamliner passed calmly over the clouds as though nothing at all had happened, and Dr Claire Casey promptly headed for the back of the plane, where she locked herself in the bathroom and vomited intermittently until it finally began to descend into the desert.

The landing was rough and arrivals surprisingly busy. Claire stumbled out of the airport with her jacket slung over one elbow and her free arm extended to pull the suitcase behind her, already feeling the effects of the cloying Australian heat. Across the sun-blistered tarmac she watched absent-mindedly as the devil-child who'd sat behind her and its mother got into a cab. She'd planned to spend a few minutes out in the fresh air before heading back into the airport to deal with the rental car paperwork, but it was cooler back inside than out here and she decided quickly to head back through the greasy glass doors and find a seat somewhere.

As she turned, she caught sight of the ambulance. The doors were wide open and a pair of female paramedics were busying themselves with lifting a stretcher into the back. Without looking too hard Claire could tell that it was the man from her flight; a flash of blue cardigan and pale, sweaty skin confirmed this.

Her own skin bristling with a thin sheen of perspiration, she turned to head back inside. The doors slid open and she wheeled her luggage over the threshold, already looking for the car rental booth so she could get the keys sorted and get out of here. There was a sour taste in her mouth and the niggling of the goosebump-scattered flesh at the back of her neck was starting to rile her up.

Her gaze locked on a young woman at the arrivals gate with a whiteboard clasped in both hands. She was fairly short, about five-four at a guess, with tanned skin and her sandy blonde hair clasped in a messy bun, the tangled arrangement of which Claire fancied wasn't entirely deliberate. Dressed in khaki shorts and a checked red shirt, the young woman's calves were exposed and Claire saw that her left leg was bandaged just below the knee. Most of the passengers had alighted and left already, but the girl was anxiously peering toward the luggage belts as if waiting for somebody. Claire had a feeling she might know who.

"Hey," she said calmly, approaching the girl. "You looking for somebody?"

The young woman glanced up at her briefly, nodded, and turned her face back to the empty airport. During that brief interaction Claire caught a flash of icy blue in her eyes, a twitch of irritation and impatience. "I'm sure he'll be here in a minute."

"I'm not sure he will be."

The girl turned again, frowning now. She could only have been early-twenties, perhaps twenty-five at most. Her neck was muscular and her arms were scratched and grazed from the desert sand. Her shirt was unbuttoned and she wore a tight white vest underneath; Claire could see the tiny protrusion of some kind of stomach piercing poking at the material. "What?"

"Old geezer?" Claire said. "Might have told you he'd be wearing a blue cardigan."

"He did, yeah… Why, has something happened? Is he still on the plane?"

"He had some kind of attack," Claire said softly. Remembering the drool and the tint to his skin, she said, "A reaction to something, I think. I had to give him CPR."

"Oh my god," the girl said quietly, finally lowering the board. The handwriting was messy and smudged.

Her accent was thick and pleasant; evidently she was from around here. "Is he okay? Is he dead?"

"He's in the ambulance outside," Claire said, pointing vaguely at the doors. "What are you, his granddaughter?"

The girl smiled thinly. "No. I called him out here to help me with something."

"Oh?"

"Doesn't matter. Just out the doors, eh?"

"I'll show you. I'm going back out there anyway," Claire lied, a little curious now. she twisted her suitcase around one-handedly and walked calmly with the girl across the airport, noticing how quiet it had gotten in the last few minutes. She supposed a small hub like this was constantly shifting from empty to bustling. "He'll be fine. They'll just have to get him to hospital, keep him stable."

"Shit," the girl said, clearly anxious about something. "Just my fucking luck."

They stepped out through the doors and the young woman hurried over to the ambulance. Claire watched from the relative shade of the building as the girl chatted animatedly with one of the paramedics, the other connecting the old man to a series of tubes. His chest was rising and falling quite regularly now; it was mostly the cracked ribs that Claire was worried about. Quickly she checked her wristwatch and cursed as she saw that it was nearly three in the afternoon. She was due at the hospital by three-thirty.

The ambulance doors slammed and she looked up to see the young woman heading her way, dismay plain on her face. "He all right?" Claire said.

"He's alive," the girl said, running a hand through her hair. Her fingers were long and slender, the webs of flesh between them crisscrossed with tiny scars as though she'd spent most of her life outdoors. "Shit. Shit, shit, shit…"

"What is it? Who is he?"

The girl looked blankly at Claire for a minute, winding both hands into the bun of her hair. Her ice-blue eyes were torn with worry. "He's a cryptozoologist. You know what that is?"

"A nut," Claire nodded. "In the field of studying imaginary creatures, right?"

The girl's eyes narrowed a little. "Right. Imaginary. Well, we called him in to help us deal with a less-than-imaginary problem. Figure he's the only one who could do anything about it."

Claire swallowed. Her eyes dropped to the bandage tightly compressed around the girl's leg. "This problem… people wounded?"

The young woman nodded cautiously.

"I'm"—*Ah, fuck*, Claire thought. The interview was in twenty minutes—"I'm a medical doctor. If there's anything I can do—"

"I'm sure you got more important things to deal

with," the girl said. "No time for imaginary creatures, right?"

With that she turned, glancing at the ambulance once more before heading across the tarmac toward a battered old four-wheel-drive across the lot, a 1990 Toyota Landcruiser with sand-scraped hubcaps and rusted rims. Claire watched her go, her heart fluttering, thoughts of Eurydice and the interview thundering through her body. This was her last chance. This interview, this job… what if they were the only ones who'd take her on, after what had happened? She couldn't fly back to England. Not after everything she'd left behind. She couldn't just give up on this.

But people were hurt.

"Shit," she murmured, fumbling in her jacket for her mobile phone and dialling quickly.

Shit, shit, shit.

"Hi, is that Dr Franklin?" she said quickly, storming across the tarmac after the young woman climbing into the four-wheel-drive. "Yeah, hello, it's Claire here. I'm so sorry, I'm gonna have to ask if we can postpone the interview. I'm so sorry. No, I know. No, no, my flight just got in, only there was somebody on board who had a heart attack, and now—"

The car door slammed. The report peeled across the tarmac like a gunshot.

"Thank you. Oh, thank you. Yeah. Yeah, I'll give you a ring as soon as I can. Thank you so much for understanding."

Shoving the phone back into her pocket, Claire dragged her luggage across the lot and hurried for the Landcruiser.

2
AFTER THE BEAR

The Toyota's suspension struggled and wheezed as the car bobbed and rattled across the desert, batted harshly by chunks of stone and solid sandy wedges of earth beneath the tyres. The interior of the car had been slowly baked for much of the morning, and now the bloated welt of the sun punched a its waxy fingers into the vehicle through the roof and the open windows, turning it into a ripe, soupy hotbox with scorching seat-covers.

Thorny devils scampered out of the way as the car thundered forward, their spiny scales shimmering as they wriggled and melted into the desert sand. A single wedge-tailed eagle flew overhead, lackadaisically circling as distant possums and feral cats limped through the heat haze on the horizon.

"I didn't catch your name," Claire called over the thumping of the Landcruiser's undercarriage, gripping the safety strap with one hand, the other folded anxiously into her lap.

"I don't remember you asking for it!" the girl said, gently steering them between hunks of sandy rock that looked as though they had been laid quite deliberately to alter their course. She glanced at Claire, taking in the older woman's dark hair, the lines around her eyes, the red marks on her sallow neck where she had rubbed her throat, then turned her eyes back to the windscreen. "I'm Sophie. Sophie Kelly."

"Good to meet you, Sophie," Claire called back.

"Ripper," the girl murmured.

"How many are hurt?"

Sophie shrugged, gripping the wheel with both hands and focusing on the trail ahead. They had left the road behind a little way back and, though the drive might have taken them an hour or two longer if they'd kept to the track, she was beginning to regret plunging them directly into the desert. But time was not on their side, and that hour might have been the difference between life and… well, the other thing. "Four of us," she said. "Sammy and Oscar didn't make it."

"What happened?" Claire said, laser-focusing on the younger woman. "Some kind of animal, I get that. I didn't realise anyone had…"

"Died?"

"No."

Sophie gritted her teeth, shifting the four-wheel-drive into a higher gear and lurching forward in her seat. "No, well. Nothing you can do for them, is there?"

"And the others? What kind of wounds are we looking at?"

"Most of them'll be fine," Sophie said. "Cuts and bruises. You might need to check them over. I'd appreciate that. But Hudson… you'll see. You got medical supplies in that bag?"

"I've got some," Claire said, glancing in the rearview mirror toward the suitcase bouncing about on the backseat. "What is it, both legs chopped off?"

Sophie shot her a look. "Something like that."

Swallowing, Claire shook her head. "And you called a… cryptozoologist? Your first thought wasn't to get this Hudson to a hospital?"

"Hudson can't go to hospital."

"Why?"

"You'll see why."

"So you were just going to leave him? If I hadn't been on that flight, you'd have—"

"Yes," Sophie said bluntly. "We called the monster hunter because he's the only person who claims to have seen one of these things before. The only person you might be inclined to believe, that is. And our priority – no offence, what with you being a medical person and all – wasn't to fix up Hudson, but to get this

31

beast paid out before it could do the same to anyone else.”

“The man who had the heart attack… he was going to help you go after it?”

“Right.”

“What now, then? You’re going after it yourselves?”

Sophie grimaced. Smiling thinly, she said, “Sure, and if you can fix Hudson up, then that’s another pair of hands. Well, another hand.”

Claire paused. For a while she watched out of the window, open a little so that some of the heat could escape without letting too much of the billowing sand inside; the horizon was a clear and cobalt blue, the white clouds she had flown above just an hour before now gone completely. “What is it?” she asked eventually. “This thing that attacked you.”

The car ploughed deeper into the desert, tyres rocking in the sand as they carved faint trenches toward the middle of the Tanami. “It’s a fucking nightmare,” Sophie said.

Hudson Ruane lay asleep in the relative shade of a hammock strung up between two desert bloodwood trunks, the wide boughs of each providing a little dappled shelter of their own. A few trees like this scattered the otherwise-sparse crater where the group had made their camp, one such specimen lying on its side, the rings of its exposed insides drizzled with dark, red sap. Hudson was twenty-two years old, Black, and handsome, usually clean-shaven but currently sporting a faint mesh of stubble across his drooping jaw. His eyes were closed and his breathing unsteady.

His right arm was missing and a chunk had been bitten out of his side. Both the grisly stump of his shoulder and the ragged pit above his hip had been dressed with crude bandages, torn shirt material wound around his midsection. Blood had oozed steadily between the checks.

The thing had ripped his arm off at the shoulder, tearing easily through flesh and bone with those monstrous molars. It wouldn't have stopped there, either, but Bugs had gotten in the way; as a result, he was sitting a few feet from Hudson with his back against the bloodwood and a hand clamped over his face, through which sticky half-congealed tracks of crimson ran down into a crisscrossed network decorating his forearm.

"Can anyone get a reception?" called a voice from the bush. Leanne was standing knee-deep in a thorny growth of spinifex grass, surrounded by saltbush shrubs. She held her mobile in both hands, aiming it toward the sun as though hoping to catch another bar of signal from the distant rays. Her hair, usually shining white and immaculately wavy, was matted to her scalp with blood – most of which was Hudson's, but the rest her own – and the back of her blouse was shredded to ribbons, exposing a back through which the creature's claws had dug four shallow, blood-red trenches. Her sleeves were gone, ripped off to provide a bandage for Hudson's stump which had quickly soaked through and since been replaced. She winced as she moved. "Hey! Anyone? I've been trying to reach Soph for the past—"

"So have I," muttered Bugs from his slack position by the tree. He glanced down at the phone in his hand, the screen cracked and useless. He clicked it open again and checked the reception. Still dead. Fucking thing.

"Pia?" Leanne called. "Anything?"

From inside one of the three tents the small group had erected – the other two were in ribbons now – a small voice offered disappointing, if not entirely unexpected, news. "Nothing," Pia yelled hoarsely. She had donated her own jacket to stem Hudson's bleeding and was largely unscathed, but she had watched Oscar's body being ripped to hunks and vomited about half of her fluid contents into the bush, leaving her woozy and dehydrated.

"Bugger," Leanne said, stuffing her phone into her pocket and turning to look in Hudson's direction. "How's he doing?"

"He's stopped twitching so much," Bugs said

quietly. "I don't know if that's a good thing."

"Come on, Soph," Leanne murmured, staring out at the horizon, a line of shimmering haze separating the vast red plateau of the desert with the electric cobalt of the sky. "Come back…"

***

Inside the tent, Pia squeezed her eyes shut and tried to forget.

She was small, her thick black hair cropped into a neat pixie-ish style that only just brushed her collarbones. Her brown skin was chipped with freckles and her otherwise-green eyes speckled with golden chits of light. She was acutely aware that Bugs thought she was pretty – in fact he had made that uncomfortably clear on the drive out here – but she'd never have agreed, nor encouraged him to carry on thinking so. In the womb-like red light that filtered easily through the pores in the canvas around her, she was little more than a trembling silhouette with angular elbows and bony knees. Outside of the tent, she felt almost equally silhouette-like – oh, god, *outside*…

Her face and neck were spattered with blood. Her *Adventures of Errol Flynn* shirt was ruined, thick pools of black having seeped through the material and stained her midsection.

She had been about eight feet from Oscar when the

35

creature had smashed his head into a damp, red-raw slab of meat on a nearby rock. She'd scrabbled desperately away, grazing her wrists in the sand, eyes widening – not fast enough to avoid the spray as the beast punched its claws into the young man's spine and ripped it out of his body.

Pia had never screamed as loudly, or for as long, as she did then. Her throat was still ragged. She felt that hours had passed before she stopped. If those headlamps hadn't exploded across the desert when they did…

She winced as pain ripped across her stomach in thick, hot bolts. Gently she tried to lift the remains of her shirt, but couldn't; the material was stuck to her, and peeling it away from her belly hurt too much. Slowly, cautiously, she slid a quivering hand inside the shirt at the back and slipped it around to feel the wound gouging her lower torso. Her fingers briefly explored the warm, softly-spilling jelly of the cavern before she quickly withdrew them.

They were going to have to leave her here, with Hudson.

She just prayed that she'd be dead by the time that creature came back to finish what it had started.

***

They'd been driving for five and a half hours when

Claire saw it.

"What's that?" she called over the rattling of the Landcruiser, pointing at a faint smudge of dark green through the windscreen. It was difficult to discern anything in detail through the glass, caked with a sandy crust of cracked red and greasy with heat, but it was evident there was something at least partly nonorganic poking out of the desert.

"Fuck should I know?" Sophie said impatiently, hardly sparing the smudge a glance. "We're nearly there now."

"Stop, stop," Claire said, leaning forward to peer through the glass. The shape was dark and angular, tucked into the rocks in the shadow of a titanic boab tree. A billowing flap of canvas near the first shape betrayed the human origins of both: a small encampment, largely destroyed by the looks of things.

"I'm not stopping for anything," Sophie said.

"I think it's a car," Claire said, her eyes returning to the dark smudge. "Stop!"

Begrudgingly Sophie slammed her heel down on the brakes and the four-wheel-drive slowed to a biting, shuddering halt. She looked in the direction Claire was looking and swallowed. "Shit," she whispered, turning off the engine. It sputtered quietly, then died. Silence filled the baking car, the effects of the air conditioning instantly dissipating. Both women stared out through the windscreen at the carnage splayed before them.

"What the hell happened here?"

Claire was already stumbling out of the car; quickly she unbuckled her seatbelt and shoved open the door, almost grateful to finally get her sore rump off that seat. Lurching forward in the sand, she looked about in despair.

Two small canvas tents were strewn about the sparse brush, only weighed down by blooms of sand that had blown into the material and formed miniature red mountains. The remains of a small collection of clothes were scattered among empty beer cans and bottles, the white ashes of an abandoned bonfire spread between them. Blood streaked the sand.

Crumpled and lying on its roof in the sand, a dark green Fortuner GX seesawed gently in the breeze. The bonnet was mangled, the passenger window shattered; a shower of glass chips lay in the sand as though the sweltering swampy heat had been violent enough to burn chunks of the billowing desert into shape. A thorny devil scampered about the carcass of the overturned four-wheel-drive, chirruping softly. The boab stood a dozen or so feet away, and briefly Claire reeled through the possibilities, but it was evident the car hadn't crashed into the enormous tree; while the bonnet was bent out of shape, the bumper had been crushed *down*, not with the impact of hitting something head-on but being smashed down into the sand itself. Something had turned the vehicle over, she decided.

Somewhere behind her, Sophie was yelling something about a body.

Claire hardly heard her. Her eyes were already fixed on the sloppy, red-raw mess of a second corpse in the shade of the boab tree.

3
REMAINS

The stench of meat was unbearable now, swampy blossoms of baked heat-smell mixing with the thick pungent tendrils of coppery blood on the air. The carcass flayed under the tree had begun to ripen, the bloody skin opening like a flower to the heat. The body had been split from head to crotch and all the insides ripped out so that they spilled into the sand, the great long cavern of the dead man's torso a blood-red explosion of organs and intestines coiling into small, heat-blistered heaps of translucent and shining tissue around him. His genitalia had been massacred, thighs shredded: the trenches ploughed through the meat of his legs were fused to the ribbons of his pants.

"Where's his face?" Sophie said dumbly behind Claire's shoulder.

Claire swallowed, her eyes tracing the bloody folds of his opened chest up a neck that had been turned inside out and was now little more than a glittering spray of cartilage. His skull was twisted to one side and his jaw and chin had been ripped off, leaving a bloody row of upper teeth sucking at the stale air. His nose and eyes had been replaced with a gory black hole through which fragments of bone and nubs of greyish-pinkish brain matter were visible. It looked like the same thing that had taken his jaw had clamped its own teeth around the rest of his face and pulled.

"There's another one," Sophie whispered, moving quickly on from her own unanswered question as though she'd realised she didn't really want an answer. "Back over here by the bonfire."

Claire turned quickly, both repulsed by the sight of the first body and optimistic, somewhere deep inside, that the second might be in a state which meant she could actually do something to help. There was no point checking the first for a pulse, nor any other signs of life; if the second was any less defiled, however, then there might be a chance for her to actually put her medical skills to use.

Her hopes were dashed the second she turned away from the boab tree and looked in the direction of Sophie's pointing finger.

The second body lay on her front in the sand, one hand plunged into the ground as though she'd been trying to crawl away. The other arm had been bent at the shoulder; bone poked through and the twisted limb lay on her back, fingers curled into stiff, slender claws. Chunks of her hair had been ripped out and her neck and shoulders were splayed into a bowl of sand-splashed viscera.

She had been torn in half at the waist and trails of spine and sloppy meat hung out of the stump of her lower torso. Her legs were spread six feet or so from the rest of her, savaged and broken.

"Jesus Christ," Claire said, stumbling back and crashing into the overturned car. She wheeled around, her boots crunching tiny shards of glass as she looked inside the ruined vehicle.

"What do we do?"

"We have to find out who they are," Claire said, bending down and reaching through the shattered passenger window. "Who they were, even. There's nothing we can do for them except let their families know that—"

She was interrupted by the sound of retching and there was a faint splash as Sophie vomited into the sand beside the first body.

"You good?" Claire called back, turning her head a little. There was a dull *kunk* from inside the car as she fumbled the glove compartment open.

Sophie nodded back, hands on her knees, body bent double. Her face was pale and her sandy hair was in her eyes. She was heaving, trying to salvage her breath. "It was the same thing," she said breathlessly. "Same thing did this... is the thing that killed Oscar and Sammy."

Claire said nothing, digging around in the spilled contents of the upside-down glove compartment. Finding a bunch of papers, she snatched them quickly and stood up straight. "His name is Dylan Wittrup," she said, glancing up from his ID. "He's a tradie."

Sophie stumbled toward her, shaking her head. "It was the same thing," she echoed. "It's out here somewhere."

"And *she*," Claire said, nodding toward the second body, "was called Michelle. Her ID is in here too. And look, there's a picture of them together."

"That's not..." Sophie started, looking over her shoulder at the photograph. "No, that's a different woman. Look, the girl in the piccy's taller than he is."

Claire looked from the drivers' license to the corpse and swallowed. "Shit."

"So there's a third body round here somewhere?"

"*Shit.*"

"Fuck. Well, we can't bury them," Sophie said, having seemingly regained her composure now. Her face was still shock-white, but her expression was determined. It struck Claire then just how young she must be; she was only slightly smaller in build than the older woman but her eyes bristled with a youthful electricity, even now. "We've no time; we've got to go and find my friends."

"We will," Claire said, dropping the IDs back into the ruined car. "You wait here a sec, I've got to go and find the other girl. Michelle."

"Why?" Sophie said. "There's nothing you can do for her. She's dead."

"She might not be," Claire said, though she was fairly confident this was more misplaced optimism.

"Fine. You've got five minutes, then I'm going to find my friends. With or without you, Doc."

Claire nodded, moving slowly through the wreckage of the small campsite. Behind her Sophie seemed to be gathering herself, and after a moment or two she started marching purposefully back to the Landcruiser. Her voice and face had realigned into the stiff, confident façade that she'd presented since Claire had met her at the airport, but she had faltered for a second, and Claire was grateful for that. It levelled the seesawing ridge between them a little.

It wasn't long before she found a chipped scuffmark in the sand, a shallow imprint where the heel of a thumping boot had wedged in the ground. The area around the scuff was spattered with blood. Levelling her gaze, Claire saw more footprints leading away, zigzagging a little, each stride long enough to indicate that the owner had been running.

Swallowing, she started to follow the trail.

From behind her came the sound of the Landcruiser's trunk opening and slamming closed, then footsteps across the ruined campsite. Ignoring them, Claire moved forward in a blurry haze, following the tracks as they veered off to the left, the blood droplets painting the scene becoming thicker and darker. Here the scuffs became a single trench, likely where the runner had fallen – or been knocked down – and landed on her side in the dirt. The trench widened into a shallow arc – she was rolling onto her back, trying to scrabble away from her attacker – and the blood was here in thick congealed smears, grains of sand painted red and glued together – and now she was clawing at the sand with one hand, staggering to her feet, and the footprints resumed, steered off to the right, scattered and frayed—

A dozen feet or so over a low crest in the sand, the remains of Michelle Iyer lay scattered across a blood-splashed scrape of desert four or five yards across.

"Oh, god," Claire moaned, clamping a hand over her mouth.

Michelle's head had been removed and it lay a few feet away in a mass of tangled, bloody hair. Her left leg was bent back on itself and a great chunk of meat ripped out of her thigh. Her left leg and both arms had been ripped off and Claire could see the chewed bones and largely untouched hands and foot half-buried in the sand around her bloody torso. Her ribs were exposed;

the creature had torn out chunks of her back. Gore spilled out of her.

Claire looked up at the sound of a chilling screech and saw a pair of wedge-tailed eagles circling the clear sky above her, hungry for the carrion at her feet.

"No," she breathed, her head swimming as she turned and staggered back to the remains of the campsite. Only now did she notice the thick, pink ropes of flesh hanging from the branches of the boab tree, swinging lazily in the breeze. She vomited, finally succumbing to the swell of nausea in her stomach.

Above her, Sophie was pumping gas from the tank in the overturned Fortuner into the Landcruiser. There was a gurgle as the oily dregs funnelled down a long, rubbery pipe.

"What are you—"

"Not much in there, but it'll get us to camp," Sophie explained half-heartedly. She looked Claire up and down. "Let me guess: you found her?"

Claire nodded, wiping her lips on the back of a trembling hand.

"I told you we needed a monster hunter for this one," Sophie said. "*Now* d'you believe me?"

Despite everything, the sun was still crawling high above them; the shade had moved.

Leanne poked Bugs in the shoulder, nodding in

Hudson's direction. The pair of them looked across at him, lying prone in the sparse spinifex grass between the bloodwoods. Bugs grunted painfully, shifting his weight a little. His hand had been clamped to his bloody face for so long that his palm seemed to be glued to his cheek; reluctantly he removed it, wincing as the congealed fluid cracked open. With his ruined eye wedged shut, he squinted into the sunlight.

"We're going to have to move him," Leanne said softly. The shadow of the hammock had shifted so that it was no longer covering Hudson's body; he had stopped twitching almost entirely now, only clenching and unclenching the fingers of his remaining hand every few minutes. Very occasionally his whole body spasmed. The blood stemming through the shirts bundled around him had mostly stopped pumping, but the heat wasn't doing the wounds of his stump and side any good.

"Fine," Bugs said. His cheek was in shreds, the squeezed-shut eye swollen and sore. The entire right side of his face was clawed from top to bottom, black and blue where it wasn't red.

Slowly Leanne stood, offering him a hand. Bugs took it and wheezed as she pulled him up, both of them unsteady. "You're burned," she said simply, and he nodded; he could feel the skin reddening, tightening, across his forehead and the top of his nose. In fact the heady sunshine had started to bake onto him like a clay coating; he felt like a golem. He was used to working long days on the farm – the idea of spending a few even-longer days out in the sun with his friends had appealed – but in his wounded haze he had evidently forgotten the importance of shelter.

The two of them shuffled over to where Hudson lay motionless in the sand. Leanne swallowed. Her father had taken her hunting more than once, and she knew the importance of ensuring that a wounded animal didn't suffer. Soon the time would come to make a decision that none of them were equipped for, that none of them had the right to make.

For now, they just had to keep him alive.

"Come on," she said, crouching at Hudson's waist and scooping his legs up in her elbows. She nodded toward the pool of shadow cast by the hammock hanging over them, now three or four feet away. "Let's get him over there."

Bugs moved to Hudson's head and slipped his arm into the crook of Hudson's remaining shoulder. With Hudson's arm missing there were limited handholds available to him, so he slid his forearm under the young man's back and splayed his fingers out wide.

On three, they lifted.

Bugs grunted; Leanne almost collapsed with the weight and the heat, but persevered. She had grown up with three brothers, all of whom were twice her size and infinitely competitive, and she'd lost count of the kangaroo and boar she'd had to drag across her father's reserve in order to prove that she was just as worthy of her place on those hunting trips as they were. She had always resented killing, but her father was such a single-minded man that she'd been forced to participate if she wanted to have any kind of relationship with him.

She wanted to kill the animal that had done this to Hudson. That had killed Sammy and Oscar…

They set Hudson down in the shadow as gently as possible, careful to angle his good arm and tip him onto his side so that the stump was raised above his heart. Leanne wasn't sure that was what was best, but he hadn't died yet, so she figured it was probably the best chance they had.

Bugs cringed, hissing with pain. She looked up, cocking her eyebrow. "What's up?"

"Just tried to open my eye," Bugs croaked.

"Don't."

"Yeah, good thinking."

He looked in the direction of Pia's tent and nodded. "Should we check how she's doing?"

Leanne paused. The sun was above and behind her and warming the wet, meaty gouges in her back. Gingerly she reached back to pluck the material of her shredded blouse and fan it softly, wincing as the breeze brushed her wounds. "She was five feet from Oscar when it ripped him in half," she said quietly. "She needs some time to herself."

"All right," Bugs said, "well, I've gotta get Hud some water. I figure he'll be able to swallow some if we tip it in his mouth."

"You think that'll make up for the hundred pints of blood he's lost?"

"Worth a try, right?"

Leanne nodded gravely and together they approached the tent in which Pia had been holed up for the past few hours. Flies buzzed about them as they moved, attracted to the blood and the sweat sticking to them. "Hey, Pia," Leanne called, "you okay in there?"

Nothing but soft, shivering breaths and feverish moans from inside the tent.

Bugs swallowed. He had said some things to Pia on the drive out to the desert that he regretted now, things that he'd wanted to say for some time but that he'd known, the second they fell out of his mouth, were wrong, were unwanted. Not that any of that mattered now. Two of them were dead; Soph was missing. He was half-blind. And that thing…

They were a few feet from the tent when it opened, trembling hands tugging the zip upward. Leanne lurched forward to catch Pia as she stumbled out, her eyes rolling up in her head.

"Jesus, what happened?!" Bugs said, freezing where he stood. Pia erupted from the tent in a mess of shaking limbs and sweat, her skin pale and covered with goosebumps, her shirt and pants covered in blood.

"I think…" Pia whispered, her head swivelling as she looked at them both through a haze. "I think I'm bleeding."

Leanne looked down. Pia's hand was pressed to her stomach, blood pumping fast between her fingers. "Oh, strewth. All right, stop moving, wait there, let's get you—"

Pia doubled over suddenly, vomiting into the sand at Leanne's feet. The stench was ripe and flowery. There was blood in it, bright red streaks dribbling through the discoloured grey fluid as it seeped between tiny chunks of stone.

"*Strewth*," Leanne echoed. "Shit, shit…"

"Sophie's back!" Bugs yelled suddenly, his eyes on a smudge of glinting metallic haze in the distance.

"Thank god," Leanne grunted, sagging under Pia's weight as the slight girl crumpled. She turned her head to watch the Landcruiser bounce toward them across the desert. "Better hope this crypto-zookeeper-or-whatever knows how to stitch somebody up."

"Get her sat down," Claire said sharply, lurching out of the car and nodding toward Pia's blood-soaked stomach. "Sophie, I need pressure on that wound. Now. Much as you can, don't stress if it hurts."

"Where the hell have you been?" Bugs yelled.

"Where's the—"

"Save your questions for later," Claire snapped, doctor-mode kicking in as she moved around to the side of the car and swung open the back door, hastily unzipping the suitcase. Already she had clocked the figure lying unconscious between the two trees and designated him priority; now as she scrabbled for her trauma kit she looked in Bugs' direction and quickly assessed his ruined face. "Can you open that?"

Bugs shook his head.

"Okay," Claire said, pulling the trauma kit loose and slamming the car door. Adrenaline pumped through her veins, a mania of frantic alertness that blotted out everything but the young men and women around her. "I'll get to you. Meantime, come help me with this."

Behind them, Sophie had joined Leanne at Pia's side and they sat her against the Landcruiser's nearside tyre, working their hands into a tight square of compression around her stomach wound. Claire caught fragments of their hissed conversation as she hurried away:

"—should have forgotten the monster and taken her to hospital—"

"—well, she didn't tell any of us she was hurt like this, did she?—"

"—even so, Hudson—"

"—Hudson can't go to hospital, you know that—"

"—and who the hell is she? What happened to your

zoologist?—"

"—*crypto*zoologist—"

Claire puffed air through her cheeks and crouched by Hudson's gently-convulsing body. Quickly she looked him up and down, clocking the crude shirt-bandages wrapped around his torso. "How many of these has he bled through?" she said.

"Uh, I… I dunno," Bugs said, "we've – uh—

"Quickly," she snapped, already working to unravel the bandage around the stump of Hudson's shoulder.

"Shit, I don't know. We've swapped them out maybe twice?"

"All right. Help me." Claire removed a selection of gauze rolls and bandages from the trauma kit and started to work. "It's a miracle he hasn't bled out. You've been keeping pressure on this?"

"As much as possible."

"He's lost about as much as he can," Claire muttered, yanking the knot tight. Hudson's whole body twitched violently. "What did this to him?"

Bugs hesitated. "I… uh, I—"

"Fine. Just help me wrap this."

Bugs crouched the other side of Hudson's body and together they wound a tight dressing around the bite wound in his side. "It just bit his arm right off," he whispered. "Took a chunk out of him here, like a shark. I've never… I don't…"

"All right. Stay calm." Claire frowned. "This

happened last night?"

"Early this morning. We were gonna… oh, god, we were gonna leave him…"

"Well, you're lucky Sophie picked me up and not some cryptid nut. What the hell were you all thinking, wanting to go after this thing? Look what it did!"

"I know, I just…"

Claire was frowning. Her eyes wandered over Hudson's bloody shirt. "What is all this shit?" she said, pressing her fingers to the material and scooping an amount of blood into her palm. She moved her hand and it swilled about, streaked with viscous, clear fluid. "Did you put something on him?"

"Eucalyptus oil," Bugs said. "Pia's idea. She had some…"

"Right. He needs to go to hospital. Somehow, between the shirts and the eucalyptus, you all managed to slow the bleeding. But that's going to get infected."

She stood quickly, grabbing the rest of the trauma kit's contents and heading back to the car. Kneeling before Pia, she gently moved Sophie's hands aside and started to apply a compression kit. As she worked she glanced from Sophie to Leanne, then back again. "You were going to leave him here? Really?"

"He can't go to hospital," Sophie insisted.

"So you keep saying. Why not?"

"Because."

"And you'd rather he'd have died?"

Behind her, Leanne was sobbing. Claire turned her head to look and saw the girl rocking on her knees, hands and forearms drenched with blood.

"What about you? Did it get you?"

Leanne shook her head. "Just my back…"

"Turn around. Let me look."

Leanne turned slowly, revealing the thick gouges across her spine.

"Jesus Christ," Claire whispered. "All right, you're next. Then the eye. And you"—glancing down at Sophie's leg, she saw the crude bandage wrapped around her calf was starting to spot with blood—"well, you're fine."

Pia gasped, sucking desperately at the air as agony bolted through her.

"Right. Stupid decisions aside, you're all going to be fine. I'm going to make damn sure of that. And we are taking you all to the hospital – whether the kid with the missing arm wants to go or not – and that's that." Claire looked up and saw that Bugs had come over to where they were huddled around the front of the car. "Can you try and open that again?"

They watched as Bugs winced, reaching up with a thumb and forefinger to ease the lids of his clawed-up eye apart. They opened to reveal the deep black pit of his socket, its edges messy with grey-pink gunk and the dried white jelly of his eyeball.

"All right. Maybe keep that closed, yeah," Claire

said. "I'll get a bandage on you in a second. Jesus. Okay. I need someone to tell me what happened. Right. Fucking. Now."

4
ATTACK OF THE GIANT KOALA

Sammy Garcia sat on her ankles by the softly-glowing remains of the bonfire, stoking it with a bent hunk of marbled wood while her crossed legs slowly died beneath her. She and Oscar had volunteered to stay up until the fire went out and make sure it didn't spread and burn down any of the tents; the flames had died a few hours ago, but the two of them had been enjoying the stars and the intermittent sounds of the wildlife around them and had decided to keep it going. It was nearly dawn.

Oscar lay sleeping the other side of the bonfire, his ukulele abandoned on a flat red rock beside him. At around three, Sammy had crept up and wrapped Oscar's blanket a little tighter around his body to stop the bugs and lizards getting in; he had since wriggled halfway out of it, but they didn't seem to be bothering him. He might have been the only one. Even before it had gotten dark, Sammy had found her legs and arms covered in bites.

Her face was low and melancholy as she watched the fire, poking it with no real intention of stirring the broken-down blackened pieces. Yellow hair fell in her eyes and she tried to keep them open, hoping to make it till dawn. Not long now; the first faint ribbons of creamy orange were splitting across the horizon. Soph had said something about driving another two hundred miles before they stopped to make camp again. Sammy was hoping she'd be exhausted enough to sleep in the car. The Landcruiser might have been the best option any of them had for going cross-country – it certainly beat her old hatchback – but it was still rough riding out in Tanami.

"Whose fucking stupid idea was this, anyway?" she murmured.

Sophie's idea. Always Sophie's idea. Most of them had known each other since they were kids, and it had always been the same. Sophie was in charge, and whatever she said just *was*. Bugs had always gone along with it, especially in their early teens when Sammy was pretty sure he'd had a crush on her. He seemed to have moved on now – poor Pia – but every now and then Sammy caught him giving Sophie a little sidelong look. Fucking creep. Oscar was easy-going, and Hudson was the youngest (though the twenty-two-year-old made up for that by towering a good four inches over everyone else). Pia was quiet, withdrawn, and she'd only known them for a couple years. But she was a good one, Sammy thought. Nice. Sweet.

Then there was Leanne. Smart, kind Leanne. Sharp-eyed, wonderful, beautiful Leanne—

"Hey," came a timid voice from somewhere behind Sammy's left shoulder. She turned her head, cocking both eyebrows.

"Hey, Pia," Sammy smiled. The younger girl's skin was a soft brown in the delicately flickering firelight, her hair a bank of shadow across her brow. Her eyes glinted like tiny white discs. "Can't sleep?"

"Kinda chilly," Pia shrugged. "Figured if the fire was still going I'd come and take advantage."

"Be my guest."

Sammy patted the sand beside her and Pia sat awkwardly, checking the ground for lizards before settling down.

For a while they sat there in silence, the minutes passing without much ceremony. Above them the sky was a blanket of inky velvet nicked with hundreds of white sparks, embers that hadn't yet burned through the material.

"It's beautiful out here," Pia said quietly, gazing up at the sky. It was hard to believe she was the oldest of them; her neck and arms were so slender Sammy wondered how her head didn't just topple off her shoulders.

"Yeah, it is," Sammy said, eyes locked on her wooden poker. She was thinking about Leanne again. Always thinking about Leanne.

"Oh, congratulations, by the way," Pia smiled, nudging Sammy softly in the ribs.

"Hm?"

"NIDA," Pia said. "Your graduation?"

"Oh," Sammy said, forcing a smile. "Yeah, I didn't graduate."

"What? I thought you said—"

"Yeah, I said I'd only come on this dumb trip if I graduated. Make it a celebration. I remember."

"What happened?"

Sammy shrugged. "Didn't work out. I put in so much time, so much work… I just didn't have what it took. And now I've got to rethink my whole life."

"Aw, no. I'm sorry."

"It's okay. I just… yeah, I thought I'd come anyway. Since I've got some thinking to do. May as well—"

Somewhere close by there was a faint squeak, the high-pitched chirrup of something swinging through the bloodwood branches. They'd picked a spot near a cluster of them, two-dozen or so trees poking out from the rough terrain like leafy stalactites. Or stalagmites.

Whichever were the *upward* ones.

"Koala?" Pia said quietly.

"Out here? Nah, I doubt it."

The fire sizzled as a bubble of sticky, boiling sap finally stretched down into the embers and ignited. A few more minutes passed and Pia's eyes fell onto Oscar's sleeping body across the fire from them. "Have you told anyone else?"

"Nah," Sammy said. "Our secret."

"Sure," Pia smiled. It'll be okay, though. "You'll figure it out."

"Thank you."

Pia swallowed. "Hey, since we're on our own out here—"

A few feet away, Oscar's throat constricted and a loud, gargling snore bubbled out of his mouth. Clamping his jaw, he rolled over. A moment later he was sleeping peacefully again.

"Since we're on our own out here," Pia tried again, her voice lower and quieter than before, "can I talk to you about something?"

"Sure."

"Something uncomfortable.

Sammy swallowed. "Is this about what Bugs said to you in the car?"

"You heard that?" Pia cocked an eyebrow.

"Yeah, I heard it. and I'll tell you right now, before you say anything else, if you're not into it, I can make sure he never says a fucking thing like that again. That's not on, Pia."

"I don't… like, I'm new to the group. I don't want to upset anyone."

"If he's saying shit like that, I don't particularly care if he gets a little upset. Understand?"

"Yeah," Pia smiled weakly. "If he… I dunno. If he says anything again—"

"Yeah, you tell me," Sammy nodded. "Or punch him. Whichever comes easiest. If he doesn't get the picture, I'm sure Soph won't have a problem with kicking him out of our little ragtag gang for good."

"Well, I don't want to—"

"Listen to me," Sammy said, turning her head and looking right into Pia's eyes. Her voice more serious now, she continued, "We don't tolerate that, okay? We don't have to, and we *don't*. It's. Not. On."

Pia hesitated, nodded, then looked back into the fire. "Hey, your stick's alight."

"Is it?" Sammy grinned, looking down at the makeshift poker. The end had caught, and a greasy hook of flame licked it violently. "*Cool.* Hey, why don't we go and shove—"

Another shrill squeak, this one louder and more guttural and echoing and right above their heads. Sammy and Pia looked up, heads tipping up in such perfectly-synchronised terror that it looked like somebody with an invisible string around each of their jaws had just yanked backward. "Oh, my g—"

It was like a great chunk of the sky fell. One second they were looking up into the top of the nearest bloodwood tree where a titanic, solid mass of black silhouette had gathered – only distinguishable from the rest of the ink-black night because it was the only portion that wasn't scattered with stars – and the next it was plummeting toward them.

The creature landed in the sand just the other side of the fire, its back rippling in the flickering light. Waves of thick, dark fur shivered between its shoulders like fields of wheat in the wind. A low cloud of dust had risen around it and it settled as the creature raised its wide head and looked in their direction, its eyes glinting wetly, pools of white reflecting in the enormous black orbs.

Slowly it raised itself onto its stubby hind legs, claws swinging as its back cracked loudly. It was the size of a bear, towering above them both. In Sammy's hand the long hunk of marbled wood had really caught ablaze and a long set of golden tendrils danced their way toward her hand. She didn't notice; her eyes were on the creature as it tilted its head to one side, then the other, flexing the bones in its squat, wide neck.

"What the fuck…" Sammy whispered.

"Is that—"

"Yeah. Giant koala."

"*Drop bear,*" Pia breathed.

Sammy glanced at her. "Wha—"

The creature shrieked, its jaws opening like a gargantuan beak in its firelit face. Its black nose shone like oil, the enormous tufted ears either side of its skull quivering as it shook its head violently. Then it turned its gaze on them again, hard, and sloughed forward, punching its claws into the earth.

"Shit."

"What the hell is that thing?!" came Oscar's voice from somewhere nearby. Sammy glanced over to see that he had woken up and rolled onto his front, and was staring at the creature with wide, horrified eyes.

Sammy didn't have a chance to reply. Before she could open her mouth the giant koala-thing was bounding toward them, its ink-black belly doused momentarily in greasy orange as it launched itself across the fire.

"Get up!" Sammy yelled, grabbing Pia by the shoulders and heaving her awkwardly out of the way. Together they sprawled into the dirt and the creature sailed past them, splaying its limbs and landing awkwardly in the sand between them and the tents. It spread its body like a dog grounding itself to shake muck out of its fur, turning in a single movement and hurtling toward them again. Sammy and Pia scrambled to their feet and staggered back, Sammy still clinging to the burning hunk of wood for dear life as the beast barrelled forward—

"Fuck off!" Oscar yelled, lurching into view. He was gripping his ukulele in both hands and there was a pathetic *twang* of snapping strings as he swung it and the wooden, miniature body of the thing struck the creature square in the head. The wood shattered and Oscar stumbled awkwardly as his body followed through, recoiling from the creature with just the broken ukulele's neck in his hand. It had stopped, apparently largely unfazed by the blow but annoyed by it. Slowly, it turned its head toward him. "Fuck," he whispered.

"Oscar!" Sammy yelled as the creature enveloped him, crossing the space between them in a second and smashing its paws into his back. There was a crunch of bone and the upper half of his body lolled backward.

Pia screamed.

The creature let Oscar fall to the ground before it grabbed him by the hair and swung his body easily, throwing it into the rock that, only moments ago, Sammy and Pia had been sitting on. Pia's hoarse yowls did nothing to stop it; as the two of them watched helplessly it grabbed the young man's head again, plunging its slick, black claws into his eyes with a faint hiss and a tiny spray of white gunk, and slamming his head into the stone. Something jolted and the meat and bone of his head realigned a little with a wet *crunch*. Pia screamed again, staggering forward, struggling against Sammy's arm around her waist. "Let me go!

It's going to kill him! It's *killing him, Sammy*!"

The beast smashed Oscar's head into the rock again and again; the boy must have fainted when his back was shattered because now he seemed to wake up, his whole body spasming as his skull was pulped. The creature's claws were buried deep in his face and blood winged around them as his temple sunk into the hard, flat plate of the rock again, again, again—

"*NO!*" Pia screamed, finally wriggling out of Sammy's grip and lurching forward. The creature paid her no mind at all, punching Oscar's head into the stone over and over, enjoying the slopping, wet sounds of the meat and bone smushing together. Chunks of brain slid down the rock as his head was flattened. Pia launched herself at the beast and smashed her full weight into it. "*YOU LET HIM GO!*"

The creature swiped back at her absent-mindedly, its claws catching her across the gut. Pia wouldn't register the white-hot pain in her midsection until a few moments later, and even then the shock wouldn't allow her to understand that it had gouged an enormous chunk of flesh out of her belly. She was thrown backward helplessly, sobbing as she smashed into the trunk of the bloodwood tree the thing had dropped out of.

It turned, lifting Oscar high in the air with one paw, its claws still buried in the mess of his face. With the other paw it grabbed his waist, and – looking very deliberately in Pia's direction with those enormous, all-black eyes — it ripped him in half like a hunk of bread, ropes of twitching intestine slopping to the floor as a gushing torrent of blood crashed into the sand.

It tossed both halves of Oscar's body into the night, the poor young man's legs seeming to kick out uselessly as they pinwheeled through the air, still spraying blood. Then it lowered itself onto all fours again and growled, wide jaw peeling back. It was bigger than a bear, Pia realised, some kind of mutant, its face the twisted snarling maw of an angry koala, its back a shivering mass of spines painted blood-orange with dark, black patches. Its ears pinned back to the sides of its skull, it slunk toward her, a gigantic mass of fur and claws with Oscar's blood streaking its yawing mouth and its powerful arms. The snarl seemed to make the sand tremble beneath her. She heard, somewhere distant, the sound of a tent being frantically unzipped, and wondered how they were only *now* being awoken by the chaos. Then she realised that it had only been a few seconds since the beast had dropped from the sky; each of those seconds had just stretched into a blood-soaked eternity in front of her.

"Pia, get back!" Sammy yelled, lurching forward with the hunk of flaming wood gripped in both hands. "Eat this, dirtfuck!"

She lunged in front of Pia and jabbed the flame into the beast's face, both of its eyes igniting with the blazing gold of the reflected flame. It growled and batted at the burning club but Sammy yanked it back, a trail of fire streaking the dark as the weapon arced back past her shoulder. Ducking out of the way of a swinging set of claws, Sammy yelled as she thrust the flame into the creature's snarling mouth.

The monster grabbed the wood with its teeth, rows and rows of sharpened molars clamping down hard, and twisted its head to throw the weapon away. Sammy fell back but she was too slow; the creature bore down on her with all its weight, punching her down into the sand and roaring in her face. A great wall of spittle and ripe, fruity heat enveloped her and she screamed as the claws burrowed into her chest, sinking between her ribs.

"Sammy," Pia screamed.

"Stay back!" Sammy croaked, trying to wrench her body from the creature's claws. It grinned savagely, blood drooling over its bottom lip, its eyes two pools of marbled infinity. The starlight on its back made every quivering spine a glinting, steel-like lance, needles of black dancing over its shoulders.

Pia howled as the beast gathered Sammy in one arm and wheeled away, bounding through the sand and into the trees. She watched in horror as the titanic shadow dragged the writhing silhouette of Sammy up into the branches of one of the bloodwoods, a spray of viscera launching into the dark like inky pellets and blotting out the stars as an awful wet rending sound echoed into the desert.

"Jesus!" Hudson yelled, straightening out of his tent and stumbling toward Pia. Behind him another shape had wriggled free of its canvas cocoon: Leanne's eyes glinted wetly in the dark as she clamped a hand over her mouth. "Pia, what the hell is—"

The beast slammed into the ground in the middle of the campsite and plunged its jaws into Hudson's shoulder. The man screamed in agony as a torrent of ichor drooled easily from his arm and with a sick twist of its head the enormous creature had ripped it free. Pia heard Sophie screaming somewhere among the tents and realised she could still hear Sammy moaning in the trees above them.

Leanne lunged for the creature and it spun around, raking its claws across her body and slamming her into the ground. It roared again, a booming guttural bellow coming from deep in its bear-like body. Soph reached to scoop Leanne off the floor and yowled as its claws glanced the back of her leg. Finally scrambling to her feet, Pia yelled and staggered toward the campsite, bending down to swipe a branch off the ground and ignoring the scratching spinifex grass at her bare ankles.

Hudson had crumpled onto his knees and the beast turned toward him, still gripping his bloody arm in its jaws. Hungrily it bore down on him, tossing the arm into the ground and looming over the cowering man, a mountain of shadow and glinting teeth.

An explosion of white light surged over the campsite suddenly, the banked beams of a pair of car headlamps swinging wildly into view. For a moment the passing car seemed to be right on top of them, rumbling across the dying bonfire like a steamroller, lights flaring violently. The beast looked up, its black eyes wide orbs of fear, then bounded back into the trees. The rumble of the car's engine stuttered as it bounced away, the headlamp beams curving off into the dark as it sped off. Whoever was driving hadn't seen them, was already too far away to stop and help. Pia looked desperately up into the trees, eyes darting from one to the next in search of the beast's great lumbering, swinging shadow.

It was gone. The sound of heavy paws thumping in the sand faded as it leapt to the ground then bounded off to the northeast.

The only shape in the trees was the limp silhouette of Sammy Garcia, hanging completely still from the branches.

5
NORTHEAST

Claire squinted into the sun, shaking her head. "I can't... you really expect me to believe this?"

Pia swallowed. Beside her, Leanne gently squeezed her hand. "It's all true," she said quietly. "I didn't see what it... what it did to Oscar, but I saw *it*. When it got spooked by those headlights, I saw it properly. Its face..."

"A giant koala?"

"Yeah," Sophie said. "A giant fuck-off koala with claws that can punch through bone and eyes like the Devil's. And we're gonna kill it."

"How?"

Sophie shrugged. "That's what Dr Brody was for."

"Dr Brody – the guy who had the heart attack?"

"That's the one."

"Well," Claire shook her head, straightening up and moving to the back door of the car, which she opened. "Shame you're stuck with me."

Rummaging in her suitcase, she sharply pulled out a wrinkled Northern Territory map and unfolded it, returning to the Landcruiser's bonnet to lay it flat.

"And the only advice I can offer is that you need to get to a hospital and away from this thing," she said, jabbing at the map with two fingers. Around her, the others looked on. She was pointing at a spot a little southwest of their current location, almost halfway between them and Lajamanu. "This is where Sophie and I found the other campsite. On our way here from the airport. There were three dead there."

She looked back at the bloodwoods.

"A couple big trees out there, too. If this thing *is* anything like a koala, then it likes the trees."

"So?" Sophie said, spitting a wadge of gum into the sand.

"So this is where it attacked you," Claire said, moving her fingers to point to the sparse, middle-of-nowhere patch of Tanami Desert where they were currently standing. She looked across the bonnet at Leanne. "And which way did it run off, when the headlights spooked it?"

Leanne pointed.

Claire nodded. "So, northeast."

"I guess so."

Claire returned her pointing fingers to the first campsite, then began to track them northeast across the map, passing through their own site before continuing across the desert. "It likes the trees and it's heading northeast," she said, "any guesses where it's going?"

"Shit," Bugs said quietly.

Claire stopped moving her fingers when they reached a patch of green beneath Tanami East. Here the Stuart Highway snaked upward through the forest, connecting a cluster of small towns. "It'll stop when it reaches the trees," Claire said, "but at that point it's not far from civilisation. And if it found you lot out here—"

"I've got friends in Elliott," Leanne said.

"This is why we have to go after it," Sophie insisted. "It killed Sammy and Oscar, it killed those three people back the way we came, and if it reaches town, it'll kill more. And what about after that? This thing's dangerous, and it's not stopping at Elliott. Can you imagine a giant koala on the streets of Melbourne? Sydney? If we don't stop it here and now, it'll—"

"It's not a giant koala," Pia said suddenly, her voice low and serious. Hand pressed to her recently-dressed wound, she shook her head. "It's a *drop bear*."

"A what?" Claire said, cocking an eyebrow.

Pia looked up. "Drop bear. You haven't heard the stories?"

"What stories?" Bug said.

"Everyone's heard the stories," Sophie said sharply. Glancing at Claire, she said, "Especially tourists. Especially *Brits*."

"Well, I didn't have much of a chance between getting off my plane and coming out here, now, did I?" Claire snapped. Turning to Pia, she said, "Tell me."

"It's a legend they tell to scare bush walkers," Pia said. "Or it *was* just a legend. There've been so few sightings that I don't know if anyone really believed the stories… so they got silly. Started telling people to spread vegemite behind their ears, then you'd be safe. That kind of thing. But if it's real…

"It drops out of the trees," she continued. "That's how it attacks. The stories say it can wait for hours, completely silent, then drop onto its prey as soon as they come within range. It looks like a koala, but it's not. It's massive, and its back is this… dark, bloody orange, with black patches. It didn't have any incisors. Just molars, strong enough to… to…"

Claire realised that Pia wasn't talking about the legend anymore; she was remembering. "Well, that's enough of that," she said, laying a hand on the girl's back. She was trembling. Looking at Sophie, Claire said, "Doesn't matter what it is, or where it's going. We need to get her – and Hudson – to hospital."

"*No,*" came a choked voice from somewhere behind them.

Sophie's eyes widened as she looked in Hudson's

direction. "Jesus," she said, lurching toward him as he tried to stand. "You're awake? Are you okay?"

She and Bugs gripped his sides, leaning him against the sun-baked body of the Landcruiser. His face was pale and sweaty, his eyes dull. He shook his head. "No hospitals."

"See?" Sophie snapped in Claire's direction.

"Why?" Claire said. "You know how dumb this is? Whatever reason you've got—"

"*No hospitals,*" Hudson insisted breathlessly, fumbling with the stump of his shoulder.

"Fine. Don't tell me," Claire said, folding up her map. She looked around the little circle of bashful faces and bruised, bloody bodies. "You want to go after a drop bear? Or do you want to get these two the help they need, and get to safety?"

"Show of hands," Sophie said flatly, her narrowed eyes on Claire. "All who want to go after it, raise 'em."

Quickly she jerked her own hand into the air. For a moment she was alone, then Hudson painfully raised his good arm.

A few seconds later, Leanne swallowed and did the same. "For Sammy," she whispered.

"Three, then," Claire said. "Fine. And all those in favour of going to the hospital?"

Pia raised a trembling hand to join Claire's. Bugs poked his up meekly, glancing at Sophie as if for approval.

"Three each," Claire said.

"Nearest hospital's Tennant Creek," Sophie growled. "Four and a half hours' drive from here."

"Then let's go."

"Three each is a *draw*, doc."

"And as the oldest – and clearly least deluded – here—"

"My car," Sophie shrugged. "You want to go, fine. You *walk*."

Claire seethed, stepping away from the car. "All right, then. You win, let's go after the monster. But I'll ask you something: what the hell are you going to do if you catch up to it? You've got no weapons. No tools. Two or three of you might just bleed out. Your tents have been destroyed, so you'll be completely exposed. And I'll repeat, just in case you didn't hear me: *no weapons*. So tell me, what's the plan?"

Sophie clamped her jaw shut. Opened her mouth a moment later. Closed it again.

"Right," Claire said. She turned to Hudson. "And you. Why can't you go to a damn hospital? You tell me, right now, or your vote doesn't count for shit."

Hudson was silent.

"Right then. Let's go. Tennant Creek, right?"

"Sure," Sophie said bitterly.

"We can pick up some stuff there," Leanne said, laying a hand on Sophie's arm. "Come out again, find it later. We'll be better prepared."

Sophie nodded. "Fine."

"Glad that's agreed," Claire said, tossing the map back into the car. "Give me two minutes to make a call."

She stormed away into the desert, fumbling for her phone and wondering, somewhere in the back of her mind, just how close Pia must have been to the creature to see its teeth in that much detail.

She saw Eurydice's eyes, coated with a pale rheum of mucus. Saw her mouth, lips dry and cracked, parted slightly. Heard her speak, her voice coarse and longing:

"Please…"

She saw the needle, glinting sharply in the flickering lights of the hospital room. Saw her own hand, trembling and pale.

Bip—

Claire circled the car for a full minute before acquiescing to the fact that her phone had no signal at all. The screen was a wash of blinding white light in the sun and an empty red box in the top corner told her that any hopes she'd had of finding some reception were fruitless.

She had a voicemail from Dr Franklin, but opening it gave her nothing. The little red box flickered with the feeble spark of half a bar as she wandered back toward the car and she froze; the only sounds that came through were bursts of squawking through a muffler of static.

"Shit," she muttered, dialling the doctor's number. That tiny sliver of reception gave her some hope, but she was reluctant to pin anything on it just yet.

The crackling dial tone was replaced by a spitting electronic voice asking her to leave a message. Certain that Franklin would only receive half of her message – if anything – she left one anyway, pinching the bridge of her nose as she spoke to relieve the dull throb of a pounding tension headache.

"It's Claire," she said, "I'm so sorry again for missing the interview earlier. The guy on the plane, turns out he had…"

She paused. Thought of Eurydice. Of all the things riding on this job. Why the hell was she risking it all for this group of monster-hunting idiots? Was she really about to lie for them, too?

"Turns out he had a family. I'm with the daughter now, she came to the airport to meet him but I didn't feel comfortable sending her back across the desert without him. I don't know if you'll get this. Listen, if you do… could we do the interview tomorrow?"

Swallowing, she looked up into the sun.

"I'm so sorry. I hope you know I wouldn't do this if I didn't have to. I… I really need this job. And I think I'd be great at it. Please, if we can do tomorrow, I'd really appreciate that. But I think I'm gonna be tied up with this girl for the rest of the day."

She glanced toward the group standing around the car, shook her head.

"And – I'm so sorry to ask – but if you could do me one more favour… could you keep an eye on the guy who came in with the heart attack? Let me know if anything happens to him. I think his name's Dr Brody. I have a feeling… it doesn't matter. Let me know. Thank you so much. I'm so sorry."

She hung up and tucked the phone back into her pocket, taking a deep breath.

When she closed her eyes, Eurydice's face appeared. She felt that it always would.

Of course, there'd been plenty that she hadn't been able to save. In her years as a medical doctor there had been more than she could count. And that was just the way it was: some she could help, and some she couldn't. Same with every doctor and patient she knew. Some could be saved, and some weren't so lucky.

But Eurydice was different.

Eurydice had asked *not* to be saved.

And Claire had listened.

Bugs and Leanne were strapping Hudson into the backseat and fumbled awkwardly with his seatbelt while Pia moved Claire's suitcase into the trunk. "Keep him awake," she called as she came back to the Landcruiser. He seemed better, despite everything, but he was far from out of the woods. If the medical shock didn't knock him out again, the loss of blood had made him weak – and she wasn't entirely certain that he really knew he was missing an arm just yet. But when he came far enough out of his daze to realise, the knowledge of that might just be enough to do him in.

"Hey," Sophie said as Claire came around to the bonnet. "Quick word?"

Claire nodded silently and followed Sophie to the ruined campsite, a couple dozen feet from the car. For a moment they stood there in silence, and while Sophie looked down at the sand between them Claire's gaze shifted from one shredded, bloody tent to another. They were running out of time, but she could tell that the girl had something to say that couldn't wait.

Eventually Sophie said, "I'm sorry."

"Why?"

The younger woman shrugged, still keeping her eyes down. "I shouldn't have dragged any of them into this. Or you. It's all my fault."

Claire paused. "What do you mean? You didn't drag them into this, you just happened to be out here when—"

Sophie swallowed. "I thought it might be out here."

"Excuse me?"

Finally Sophie looked up, her eyes dark and regretful. "I told them it would be nice to take a few days out in the desert. Oscar needed a break from work, same for Leanne. Pia said she wanted to get to know everyone a little better. Sammy just graduated. I thought… I said, why don't we take a trip? Brought them all out here, said we could just spend a few days away from it all."

"And you didn't tell them you thought there might be a man-eating koala out here," Claire said flatly.

"I didn't know if it would be, not really. But I heard… I saw it, you know. When I was a kid. It… oh, god. Look, I'm just… I'm sorry."

"What the hell were you going to do if you found it? Did you bring any weapons? Anything?"

Sophie blinked. "I didn't think," she said, shaking her head, and Claire saw that she was near tears. "I figured it couldn't actually be real. And if it was… well, I thought we'd just outrun it in the Landcruiser."

"Oh, you didn't think it might attack at night, while you *weren't* in the car?"

"Look, I'm trying to… I made some mistakes, okay? I put everyone at risk. I called that dumb fucking cryptozoologist because I thought he could come meet us out here, I thought he could *help*…"

"And when it came," Claire said, "when it ripped your friend's arm off—"

"Yes," Sophie said quietly. "I could have gone to

get a doctor. I could have taken everyone to get help. Whatever. Brody's flight – your flight – was coming in, and he'd be there by the time I got to the airport… I figured he'd have medicine. Better still, something to fight this thing with. I made a decision."

"Bad call."

"Yeah. Fine. But we got you, anyway, didn't we? Proper doctor. And now Hudson's going to be fine—"

"Hudson's missing an arm and all we've done is stop him losing any *more* blood," Claire said. "And even that isn't definite. You know he has to see someone, right? Or your friend might actually die. Same for Pia. They need help."

"I know."

Claire shook her head. "Look, I get it. People don't think clearly when shit happens. And this… what happened here… this was some *shit*. But you have to tell them. You have to tell them you knew it might have been out here. And I'm not snitching, I'm not saying turn yourself in. I'm not saying you need to tell them because it'll help *them*. But if you keep that to yourself… it'll burn you up inside, Soph. It'll eat you. Guilt like that, *secrets* like that… they have teeth."

Sophie cocked an eyebrow. "You got secrets, doc?"

"I got some." Her stomach twisted into a tight knot and she laid a hand on Sophie's arm. "Tell them."

"Yeah," Sophie said. "Anyway, I… I'm sorry. Let's forget the monster and go fix everyone up."

Before she could walk back to the car, Claire said, "What happened?"

"Huh?"

"When you were a kid. When you saw it before. What happened?"

Sophie smiled thinly. "It ate everyone," she said simply.

"Everyone?"

"I was six years old," Sophie said. "I lived with my parents and my brother. Mark. Me and him shared the attic room. It was huge. Stretched across the whole top of the house, and the rafters sloped up into the middle so that you couldn't really see the whole ceiling. It was like this big well of shadow right above us.

"That's where it came from. I don't know how it got in. Or how long it was waiting there. But I remember watching as it dropped from the ceiling and landed on my brother's bed. He was three years older than me. And it… it ripped him in half. It was smaller, back then. I don't know if it would have been the same one. Can't have been. Either way, it was younger. A juvenile, I guess. I thought it was just a regular koala, except it ripped him open like some kind of rabid dog. I screamed. I didn't know what to do, but I lurched out of bed, went forward—

"And then he was gone. The weight of the thing and my brother was too much for his bedframe. It must have been real heavy. The attic floor couldn't take it –

it caved in. they fell through.

"I had to watch from above as my parents came out into the hall and it tore out my dad's throat. My mum was next. For a moment I was right above them looking down, and I could smell the blood and the meat as it ripped them inside-out… I remember thinking, is this what *it* did? Did it just… watch us from above? And maybe I could drop down – it had forgotten all about me, I was sure of that – so maybe I could steal its signature move, you know? Jump down onto its back, it was only my size, maybe a little bigger… but I didn't. I just crouched, watching. Useless."

"There was nothing you could've done," Claire whispered.

"Well, now there is," Sophie said, gritting her teeth. "I don't care if it's the same bastard thing or not. Soon as this lot get the help they need, I'm coming back out here and I'm gonna kill it."

Claire nodded. "Okay."

"You across that now?"

"More than."

"Good," Sophie said, turning for the car. "Let's go."

Claire waited until Sophie had reached the Landcruiser before she let out a shaky breath, surprisingly broken up by what the younger woman had told her. Tearfully she looked around her, eyes moving slowly across the ruined tents. Scraps of blood-matted orange fur were twisted around the thorny needles of the saltbush shrubs, thin ropes of blood hanging like drool into the sand.

Something glinted in the mess of torn canvas and bloody sand at the foot of the nearest bloodwood tree.

Frowning, Claire moved toward the thing, bending down into the sand to scoop the thing into her palm. Turning it over, she cringed as knots of damp fur trailed between her fingers.

She was holding a clump of furry flesh, gobs of congealed red blood clinging to it. Presumably the creature had wounded itself at some point; this was a small, scrappy hunk of the drop bear, a sliver of leathery skin riddled with splinters and tiny glassy flecks of sand.

And sewn into the flesh, the size of a small coin, was a metallic tag of some kind, so small that she had to squint to see it. As she twisted it in her hand, the sunlight caught and glinted sharply.

Embossed on the tag was some kind of logo that looked like a sprawled gecko, its blobby limbs splayed out, its tail curling around to its snapping maw to form a crude circle.

Claire thought about pocketing the thing, then remembered just what she was holding, grimaced, and tossed it back into the sand.

It was probably nothing.

6
FROM ABOVE

The desert was quiet and calm, sand shifting lazily over layers of sand: a great red onion constantly peeling and unfolding itself only to repair those broken coats when the wind changed. The wind itself was little more than a slow pulse that ruffled the dunes and did its best to stir the leaves in the sparse, if miraculously well-fed, boabs scattered about. Around a small and shallow pool of glittering blue water, a small herd of wild camel milled aimlessly about each other, mothers nudging their young toward the miniature oasis to encourage them to drink, protective bulls chewing half-heartedly while their lazy eyes roamed the plains. The Australian heat seared scabby, matted fur and insects danced across the tufted mountains of their humps, occasionally batted away by shabby tails.

About sixty yards away sat a beige, beaten Ford Everest, the bonnet baked into a spatter of peeling metal and paint so that it looked as if it had been splashed with acid. The driver's side window was open, and something long and dark poked out. The rest of the windows were tinted so that from a distance it was impossible to see inside. The car was parked in the shade of a leafy boab, its trunk almost as wide as the car itself and only twice as tall.

Noah Murphy was sprawled comfortably in the backseat, drinking greedily from a two-litre bottle of water before drizzling a little into the collar of his open shirt. He was a large man and his forehead was laced with sweat, more of it staining his clothes. An unloaded field-weight Finnfire 94 was nestled between his feet and a bulging Hessian sack lay beside him on the seat, a pair of towels spread beneath it so that the blood didn't seep into the upholstery. The inside of the old Ford stank to high heaven: the ripe, fresh stink of recent kills knitted into the blossoming cloud of body odour and testosterone and pooled across the ceiling before spilling down again.

In the driver's seat, Sam Stewart was sat with his body twisted to the side and his own hunting rifle thrust out of the open window, one eye closed while he watched the camel through the scope with the other. His weapon of choice was a .223 Highlander M85 – good for feral cats, wild dogs, and kangaroos – and he gripped it gently, finger curled around the trigger but not quite touching it. The butt of the rifle was clamped neatly in his shoulder and though his steady breathing slowly jerked the .223 up and down, wheeling the crosshairs ever-so-slightly over the drinking cow's body, he was acutely aware of these movements and knew just the point during that arc when he would squeeze the—

"Christ, are you going to fucking shoot one yet?" Noah moaned from the backseat, rummaging in a bag in the footwell and loudly withdrawing a packet of something that stank like stale salt and vinegar.

"Shut up," Sam murmured, readjusting his grip on the rifle. Noah had been proudly plucking hares from the sand with his Finnfire all morning and boasting the fact that Sam hadn't made a single kill; Sam had been forced to remind him a few times that his .223 would have taken the head clean off anything as small as that.

Now they had finally found some big enough game, he was damn well going to have his turn.

Slowly he drew a bead on the bull's head, following it carefully as it ducked into the water and swung upward again. The camel stood proudly among the herd, its neck dashed with tiny sparks of black that crawled incessantly into its fur. Sam would have to be quick: once the first shot went off, they would all dart. But he'd picked out his second shot, and he had a pretty good idea which way she'd run. Focusing again on his breathing, he pressed his finger lightly to the trigger.

"Come *on*!" Noah complained, slumping forward and knocking Sam's body and the rifle out of position. "Jesus, you're killing me, man!"

"For fuck's sake, will you shut up for more than fifteen seconds and let me do this?" Sam snapped impatiently, elbowing Noah off the back of his seat and getting back into position.

"Fine," Noah pouted, slamming his body back into his seat and rocking the car. "Yeah, you carry on, man. You carry right on…"

Gritting his teeth, Sam returned his eyeball to the scope and prepared to fire. The bull hadn't moved, and it didn't take him long to settle his breathing again and ready his finger on the trigger. "Right," he said softly, more to himself than Noah, "I'm on it. No more interruptions…"

Something dropped onto the roof of the car with an enormous *thwump*. The four-wheel-drive shuddered on its axels and Sam's finger hammered the trigger, firing a wild round into the middle of the herd. The bullet smacked the sand and a cloud of it blossomed, camel bleating and barking as they scattered.

"Shit!" he yelled, his eyes shooting up to the ceiling. The car was still shaking as he slammed back the bolt and repositioned himself, swinging the barrel of the .223 in a desperate arc. It was useless; the camel were bolting. "Shit, Jesus—fuck!"

"What the hell was that?" Noah said in the backseat. Water was spilled all across his shirt.

"How the fuck would I know? Probably a branch or some shit. Oh, for fuck's sake."

The car had stopped shuddering. Whatever had dropped onto the roof wasn't moving. Noah looked up and saw that the weight of the thing had punched a shallow dent into the ceiling. "Yeah," he said quietly. "Just a branch."

"Go out and look if you're worried about it," Sam growled, fumbling in the glove compartment for a map. "Hurry up, though, I want to get moving again."

"You look."

"Look at what?" Sam snapped. "There's nothing out there, dickhead."

"Fine." Noah crossed his arms, huffing as he settled back in the seat.

A moment passed before Sam turned his head, seething. "Well? You're not bothered, now, then?"

"Like you said," Noah grumbled. "Nothing out—"

The thing on the roof shifted.

The car rocked again as it moved from the front of the roof to the back, the distinctive sound of clawed, clacking paws echoing above their heads. Instinctively Sam wrapped a hand around his rifle.

"Go look," he whispered.

Noah shook his head. "*You* go."

"Fine," Sam grunted, pedalling the heel of his hand

into the doorhandle and crushing it open. He turned awkwardly and scrambled out of the car, kicking up a small cloud of sand as he landed. Rifle nestled in his shoulder, he took a step forward and turned, looking up at the roof of the four-wheel-drive.

Inside the Ford, Noah watched through the tinted window with his heart in his mouth. Blood pumped loudly in his ears as Sam paced across, swinging the rifle left and right as he surveyed the roof. After a moment he leered down, knocked loudly on the window, and jeered.

"Nothing up there!" he called, and Noah's heart settled a little. "Probably just a—"

Sam screamed as a streak of grey and orange lunged down from above and slammed into his shoulders, dragging him up into the air. A great wing of blood splashed the window and Noah shrieked with terror as the thing on the roof launched its weight into Sam's body and punched another dent into the roof.

They ploughed through the desert, Sophie and Claire in the front of the Landcruiser and the others crammed tightly into the back. It was uncomfortably hot and stank of blood, and at the speed they were barrelling over the sand it was impossible to have any of the windows open without enormous clouds of it coming in.

"How far are we now?" Pia called from somewhere in the huddle of bodies on the backseat, sandwiched awkwardly between Bugs and Leanne. Her face was pale but the dressing on her stomach wound seemed, at least, to have stemmed the bleeding for now.

Sophie glanced into the rearview mirror, swallowing when she saw the colour of Hudson's face. They had kept him awake this long – it would have been hard to fall asleep, with the stump of his shoulder practically glued to Leanne's arm through the bloody bandages – but he was evidently fading. She couldn't believe she had been so stupid. Could they really have just left him there? Shaking her head, she said, "Hour at most. Nearly there, guys."

"Sit back," Claire said, turning her head to look back at Leanne. The younger woman had been hunched forward for the last half hour, trying to avoid pressing her shredded back against the baking upholstery. "The pressure is good."

"Easy for you to say," Leanne murmured, but she wrestled herself backward.

Claire glanced in Sophie's direction. The girl's knuckles were bone-white, pressing up against her flesh as she gripped the wheel. "You good driving? Need me to take over?"

"I'm good," Sophie said, hardly flinching as the car barrelled over a rocky outcrop and shuddered harshly. Behind them, a blossom of red-white sand slung itself across the horizon and caked the rear window. The sun was beginning to fade, rolling down a steep hill of pink-purple cloud into the distance.

The Landcruiser sputtered and Claire's eyes flickered to the dash. "How we doing for fuel?"

Sophie shook her head. "We've got enough," she said, though Claire couldn't help but noticed that she had slowed the car to somewhere between fifty-five and sixty miles per hour.

She returned her eyes to the windscreen and frowned as she saw a faint orange smudge growing larger and closer. "What's that?"

"Dingo," Sophie said simply.

"You're not going to hit it, are you?" Claire said, baulking at the speed at which the smudge was growing. Now it was less than sixty yards away and she could make out the shape of a mangy, muscular wild dog, its ears pressed back against its canid skull, its fur golden and shimmering with heat.

"No, I'm not going to hit it," Sophie grunted, steering to the left just as Claire caught a flash of the dingo's yellow teeth. "You think I'm just going to drive into a—"

She yanked the wheel suddenly to the right as another wild dog lurched toward the windscreen.

"Jesus," Sophie hissed, trying to bank the car back toward the road. "Pair of them…"

Claire turned her eyes forward as the younger

woman trailed off.

Behind them, Leanne swore.

A pack of dingoes had spread themselves across the horizon, some just prowling orange dots in the heat haze, some closer and hunched, their eyes trained deliberately on the car. "Where the hell did they come from?" Claire said, amazed.

Sophie shook her head, glancing into the rearview and spotting a couple more dark shapes through the mire of dirty sand on the glass. "They're all around us," she said. There were more to the right, too; they seemed to be stalking the car as it moved, some of them sprinting across the sand to keep up, others appearing out of the sand as though they had been burrowed beneath it.

"Just keep going," Leanne said. "They won't attack. We're safe in here if they do."

Sophie swallowed, squeezing the pedal with her foot and punching the Landcruiser forward. They were heading right into the middle of the pack, carving a trail out of the sand as they cruised unevenly over the dunes. Sharp ears perked up on lowered heads as dingoes rose from the ground and stalked over the horizon, slinking toward the approaching car. Claire saw black lips peeling back over sharp, yellow teeth, eyes narrow and focused. They were the size of wolves, flea-bitten and scabby, bodies sleek and powerful.

"Turn," Claire said.

Sophie kept pushing forward, heading for a narrow valley through the oncoming pack, her teeth gritted in a hard, square jaw. More and more dingoes were appearing all around them, leaving an opening on the left but otherwise surrounding the car. Teeth flared in the heat, sharp eyes glinting.

"Turn. Sophie—"

Something slammed into the side of the car and Pia screamed as a thick, dark shape blotted out the windows.

"*Sophie, turn!*"

Sophie yanked the wheel down to the left as another dingo leapt onto the bonnet, punching its paws into the metal and leering down into the windscreen. As the car veered sharply the dog was thrown off, and it sprawled in the sand with a rumbling growl before slinking after them. "There's so many of them!" Sophie yelled.

"There!" Claire cried, pointing forward. A pathway lay open before them, narrowing every second as the pack closed in.

"They're herding us," Pia whispered.

"Don't be dumb," Bugs said, squinting with his good eye, the rest of his face obscured by a blood-spotted dressing tied tightly at the base of his skull, "they're wild animals, they don't—"

"No, she's right," Claire said, watching out of the window as the Landcruiser crashed across the shallow dunes. All around them, dark smudges prowled forward, slinking through the shimmering heat haze as they wheeled on the car. Working in formation, pedalling them north. "They are herding us."

"They can't be."

Another wild dog smashed its body into the side of the car and Sophie veered to the left, yelping as she twisted the wheel. "I reckon they might be!" she said. "What the hell is going on?"

"I don't know," Claire said weakly.

Outside, the sun was dragged on invisible ropes down toward the welcoming arms of a pink-tinged horizon.

The Ford sagged heavily on its axels as the weight on the roof shifted, a series of thumps and rattles booming throughout the interior. "*Jee*-zus!" Noah yelled, grabbing his Finnfire and rolling for the door, slamming it open.

He hit the sand in a heap, the Ford crashing backward behind him and tumbling onto its side. He reeled onto his back and looked up to see a streak of blood-smeared sky pealing away from him. Scrambling back, he loaded the rifle and jammed it into his shoulder, swinging the barrel upward.

"Come on, you big kanga-fuck!" he cried, backpedalling from the overturned four-wheel-drive. Coughing as blooms of sand invaded his throat, he steeled himself and listened.

Before he could draw another breath something was thrown over the top of the car toward him, spiralling through the air as a pink-grey smudge. Noah tracked the thing quickly and squeezed the trigger without thinking, his finger working on autopilot. A spray of clotted red exploded from the thing as it skittered into the sand.

"Take that!" he grinned, reloading quickly and looking down at the broken thing.

His smirk faded and nausea swelled in his throat as he realised he was looking at Sam Steward's bloody head. He had shot a small black hole into the temple and the back of the skull had exploded, ribbons of brain matter streaking the sand. Sam's eyes were open and terrified, his jaws slack around the yawing black hole of his mouth. The head rolled between Noah's ankles, blood oozing from a ragged hunk of neck encasing lumps of greasy, exposed cartilage.

"Oh, shit," Noah said, vomiting as he scrambled to his feet. Suddenly dizzy, he whirled around as another sound came from behind the car. He raised the rifle and swallowed, cringing at the acrid taste.

The beast rose up from behind the mangled wreck of the Ford and blotted out the sun, its titanic shoulders beading with tiny halos of light.

"Oh, *shit…*"

The creature was titanic, a mountain of blood-spattered fur and muscle. It clambered onto the car and beat its chest with one fist, the folded claws glittering black in the sunlight. The clicking sound that erupted from its throat was followed by a piercing shriek, and Noah caught a flash of blunt, hammer-like teeth. It was the size of the Ford, for Christ's sake. Bigger, even. And in the other hand it was holding Sam's headless body, gripping it by the shirt, blood flooding from the stump of his neck. It wasn't a kangaroo like he'd expected: the thing was a giant koala. Its legs were stumpy, the fur around its ankles and calves thick and twisted and dirty. Its torso was squat and spines of orange-black fur shivered on its shoulders. Thick wedges of fur sprouted from its great flat ears.

Noah Murphy lifted the Finnfire and squeezed the trigger again, the dry report of the rifle booming around him as a plume of gunsmoke barrelled forward. The bullet smacked the creature in the shoulder and ripped loose a small hunk of furry flesh; the beast seemed not to notice.

Its jet-black eyes narrowed angrily and it dropped Sam into the sand behind the car, flexing its claws. The beast's enormous shadow hung over Noah, a welcome bank of shade in the heat – if only it were cast by something that wasn't also staring at him so intensely that his blood had turned to ice—

Fumbling, he reloaded and fired again. The drop bear screamed sharply as the bullet punched into its belly and bounced off – then it surged forward, launching itself off the vehicle and toward him.

Noah screamed as the creature slammed him into the sand, plunging its claws into his stomach and ripping out something warm and wet and flailing. Ropes of intestine glistened at the edges of his vision as blood splashed his face. He barely registered the pain. "What… are… *yo—uuuuuu—*"

His words were twisted in his throat and became a wet, slopping scream as the creature bore down on his neck, clamping those stony teeth into his flesh and pulling hard. Somewhere he heard the bleating of a wild camel as the drop bear punched its teeth into his ribcage, cracking it open easily. Then everything faded to an awful orange-black and the last thing he heard was the dreadful wheezing *schlop* of the creature drawing his deflated lungs into its furry beak.

The drop bear feasted for a while, returning to its first kill when the meat of the second had been depleted. The camel had dispersed and the only sign of movement for miles was the lumbering gait of the mountainous, gore-streaked silhouette as it lurched up onto the wreck of the Ford and looked into the sun.

Eventually it turned and continued northeast, heading for a thin strip of silhouetted treeline in the distance.

7
TREETOPS

A thick purple blanket of dusk stretched over the horizon, bulging where thin wisps of pink-blue cloud clawed at the last scraping strikes of sunlight. The sun itself was faded fast, a once-bloated and raging orb deflated and sickly as it rolled downward. The desert buzzed with the breaking heat as lizards and birds stalked slowly across shallow dunes.

The Landcruiser headed steadily toward Elliott and Newcastle Waters. A slick sheen of water lilting off the sand, a strip of shining haze that Sophie had told the others was the Lake Woods Conservation Covenant national park, glittered with the soft hues of late evening; beyond it, a sparsely-wooded stripe of land was growing ever closer. The trees were tall and bushy, each one poking quite unnaturally out of the sand to form a sort of almost-forest.

Behind them, a pack of dingoes chased the car at top speed. There were dozens of them. One would snake in from the side of the vehicle every now and then only to snarl menacingly at the four-wheel-drive before joining the pack following it across the desert.

"How long have they been following us like this?" Claire said, watching the dogs in the rearview mirror. Occasionally they would slip back into the desert, but there were periods where the Landcruiser clipped along over particularly severe terrain and the wild animals started to catch up again. They were a prowling menace, slow but unrelenting.

"Too long," Pia said in the backseat, her neck turned so that she had a clear view through the sand-caked rear window. Beside her Bugs shifted uncomfortably, clearly suffering a lot of pain at the claws of his congealed facial wounds.

There was no hope of rediverting the car toward Tennant Creek now, not without steering right through the pack. The sharp-eared creatures looked somewhat larger than those Sophie Kelly had seen before, and as she drove she couldn't help but notice that their muscular shoulders and necks were thicker; even their skulls seemed larger, sleeker. Yellow-gold fur was painted pink by the fading sun and patchy with the dirt of the outback and the crusty, sharpened twists of mange that was apparent, too, in their savagely-glinting eyes.

There was something different about them.

"I've never seen a pack this big," Hudson murmured, his words slurred and uncomfortably drawn-out. It was evident that he was becoming more and more tired, and with the hospital growing farther away with every passing minute, Claire was starting to worry that it was already too late. She kept quiet, encouraging the others to keep him awake. There was no sense in telling them that he might not last the night.

And what if none of them did? She was aware now that she was about to share her first night in the Tanami Desert with a group of injured strangers and an angry koala. And now the pack…

"They're slowing down," Bugs said after a while, frowning into the rear window. Pia nodded beside him. half an hour or so had passed since the most recent surge of thudding paws and clamped, slavering jaws; either they were growing tired, or something else was going on.

"I wonder why," Claire muttered, watching as the smudges on the horizon began to fade into dots, and then into particles, and finally into nothing. They were driving through empty desert now, clumps of brush forcefully grabbing at the tyres, the dingoes seemingly bored with their chase.

Sophie began to slow the car. "I think I know why," she said quietly.

"They really were herding us," Claire breathed, her eyes forward. "I can't believe it."

Three or four miles away, the sparse trees began to loom, a row of crooked sentinels with leaf-armoured shoulders, lanky arms spreading into vicious gloved claws above. The darkening fingers of the sky painted silhouettes between pale trunks and knots of viny spinifex grass; in the oncoming dark, the trees became a thick woodland. A narrowing stretch of sand separated the Landcruiser from the approaching trees, the last thick stripe of flatland before they sped right into the long-toothed mouth of the dark.

The dogs had led them – *forced* them – right to the exact spot on the map where Claire had imagined the drop bear would make its home for the night. They had led them to *it*.

"What the hell is happening?" Claire whispered.

Save for Hudson's laboured breathing and the low rattle of the engine, there was silence inside the car. Nobody had an answer.

The woods were dark, and there was something moving in the trees.

Far away there was the sound of an approaching four-wheel-drive; this was the sound, in fact, of a beaten 1990 Toyota Landcruiser, which at this very moment was beginning to slow as the creatures dogging it pealed back into the sand. The shallow roots of the trees made the desert at their feet lumpen and hard, and a thin scattering of dead leaf material blew lazily across the shallow trenches dragged through the ground by skinks and mulgara.

Branches groaned as something shifted among them, an enormous weight knotting up into the canopy and lumbering from tree to tree. Its shadow was an extension of those cast by the trees themselves, hardly discernible from the banks of shade they cast. Its movements were somehow lithe and elegant despite its size and weight; if one had not been listening, one would never have known it was there. Out in the desert, the Landcruiser's engine sputtered and stopped. Silence.

A dry crunch sounded from the edge of the woods, the report of something snapping.

A moment's pause, and then the whisper of a shadow passing between two trunks. Something moving at ground level, something smaller than the beast up in the treetops.

Slowly three shapes filtered into the trees, the very last of the sunlight riding the polished barrels of three semi-automatic rifles, swinging lazily left and right. The figures were human-shaped but covered in black padded armour, shoulders and chests strapped into pebbled Kevlar vests. Heavy boots clumped in the sand as they moved cautiously forward.

"Sure we'll find it here?" said one of the figures quietly, a muffled female voice escaping the dark visor of a round black helmet. Naomi Lee gripped the rifle with gloved hands, her slight figure bulked out by the thick paunches of her uniform. Reaching up quickly to dial on the night vision built into her visor, she glanced up into the canopy before taking another step into the sparse, yet overwhelmingly claustrophobic, knot of the trees.

"The tracker sent out one last signal before it was bust," said the second figure, a tall, narrow man with the scruff of a black beard faintly visible where his throat was exposed. "No reason to think it wouldn't head for the nearest woodland."

Hunched over to grip his rifle, Armstrong moved not like a soldier but more like a hunter: Naomi supposed he would have been, given the choice.

Oh, choice. What a thing. If *choice* had ever come into it, then she wouldn't be here either.

"Quiet," said the third soldier, a few steps ahead. Joey was broad-shouldered and filled out his armour nicely, the padded pockets of his combat trousers bulging against the strain of his muscular legs. Lifting his visor, he revealed eyes that were usually ice-blue but, in this half-light, appeared as two faint silver discs. Looking all around, he gestured with a knife-like hand for the small group to press deeper into the woods.

The sandy floor was alive with tiny insects which

had made their homes in labyrinthine burrows beneath the tree-roots and in small piles of decaying organic matter all around them. At the base of one tree the broken skeleton of a rotted bustard had been sucked so ravenously of any remnants of flesh and hair by starving carrion birds that it was ivory-white and glistening.

Naomi peered through a haze of greenlit bands of static, the tall and leaning pillars of trees patched through the glass in banks of heat for her to peer through. "Could be anywhere," she breathed, her heart pounding loudly in her ears. "Have either of you seen this thing before?"

"Joey here put the tracker on it himself," Armstrong said, gesturing vaguely at the third figure with his semi-automatic. "Hey, Joey. Did you install the inhibitor, too? Or was that something for Johnson's department?"

"Inhibitor?" Joey said quietly, swinging his rifle slowly and eyeing the faint red dot that tracked through the scarce wall of trees before them. "You think everything that comes out of The Cage gets an inhibitor?"

Naomi cocked an eyebrow, the blank slate of her visor remaining outwardly unchanged. "Don't they?" she said. "Why not? Surely it would be better if we were able to—"

"Wouldn't be much point in the project, now, would

there?" Joey said impatiently. "If everything it produced could be stopped. We need things that keep going, no matter what kind of signals get thrown into their brain. Things that don't ever stop. That's the whole point of the project, dummy. That's the only way we win."

"You really believe it, huh?" Armstrong said, lowering his rifle a little. "All this shit about the Bluetongue—"

"Quiet," Joey hissed. "Both of you."

They progressed for a little while, melting into the shadows as the sun tilted back over the horizon and the last bands of deep red began to disperse. Armstrong couldn't stop himself from cringing every time the treetop whistled or rustled above them. It was out here somewhere, he knew. But where—

Naomi froze in the shadow of a tall, leaning tree, her body stiffening. Armstrong noticed the change in her movements in the corner of his visor and turned his head, following her gaze. She was looking directly at the trunk of the tree in front of her. At first he couldn't figure out what she was looking at, but when he took a cautious step closer he saw it.

"Shit," he whispered. "Boss…"

Joey turned his head, immediately pinpointing the others. He nodded.

Armstrong gestured toward the tree. Naomi, still frozen still, swallowed nervously.

The trunk was clawed open, deep trenches carved from it where sharp sets of claws had burrowed through the bark. Sharp chips and splinters of wood exploded outward from the centre of every wound, long scrapes dancing between thick, pale gouges.

Slowly Naomi turned up her head, following the claw-marks as they climbed the trunk into the canopy.

"There," she whispered, and then something snapped far above them.

8
FIRST WATCH

They were half a mile or so from the trees when the Landcruiser ran out of gas.

"Shit," Sophie muttered, stamping on the accelerator as the engine began to sputter, the choking four-wheel-drive stuttering to a halt in the sand. "Shit, shit, shit…"

"I thought you swiped some gas from that Fortuner," Claire hissed, checking all the windows for movement as the car died with a loud, wet cough and sank onto its axels. Briefly she recalled one summer in the Scottish highlands where her father had been hunched over the open bonnet of the family car, sweat running in little rivers through the cracks of his face, grease all over his hands. The smell of smoke and fresh-mown grass had almost pervaded her terror at the angry look on his face. By that point in her life it had become very familiar.

"Well, clearly they didn't have a full tank either," Sophie said. It was dark outside and difficult to see, but the desert stretched soundlessly away from them; the dingoes that had hounded them forward seemed to have gone, for now. "We're gonna have to go on foot."

"Where?" Pia whispered.

"If we can get through those trees, we'll get to Elliott," Sophie said. "They might be able to put us up."

"Or we could avoid the trees and head for the road," Claire said, leaning to open the door. Fumbling quickly in the glove compartment, she was relieved to find a bulky flashlight and grabbed it triumphantly. As she lurched out of the vehicle Sophie and Bugs followed her out onto the sand, doors slamming behind them. "We can't go in there in the dark," she continued. "It'll slaughter us. But if we can go round…"

She clicked on the flashlight and aimed it vaguely west, illuminating a stretch of cracked tarmac road a few miles from the dead four-wheel-drive.

"Shit," Sophie said again.

The torchlight rolled smoothly over a collection of haggard shapes on the road, dark stiff-shouldered smudges that they knew, even from this distance, were watching them. More wild dogs, their pointed ears warning signs protruding from sleek, vicious heads.

They sat and lay on the tarmac, a couple pacing calmly. Waiting.

Claire swung the torch beam as Leanne and Pia helped Hudson out of the car, shining it into the desert all around them. More faint shapes lingered on every horizon, hanging back but close enough that she felt she could hear them slavering hungrily.

"They've pushed us this far," Claire said quietly. "If we don't go into those trees, they're going to keep pushing."

"We can't," Sophie said. "Like you said, if it's in there…"

"It'll rip us apart." Claire turned her head, frowning. "You've changed your tune."

"Saw some sense, I guess. What do we do?"

"I wanna nap…" Hudson murmured, almost drunkenly.

"No," Pia said, shaking him a little. "No, you stay awake, now."

"We can't do anything till daylight," Leanne said, her eyes steely. Claire clicked off the flashlight and the desert around them became a pall of shadow, the sky above an equally suffocating blanket of star-sprinkled oily blackness. "They've stopped chasing us, right?"

"They know we can't go back," Claire realised. "As soon as we try, they'll come for us."

"Well then, let's not try," Bugs shrugged, wincing as the muscles of his face contorted painfully beneath the bandages. "Maybe they'll stay back if we don't try to run."

Claire swallowed. "We'll have to go through those trees in the morning."

"Better than doing it now," Sophie said.

"Yeah," Claire nodded. "Rather camp out here than in there, right?"

"Right," Bugs agreed, his bandaged face a ghastly white mask in the moonlight. Leanne nodded forcefully.

Sophie glanced in Hudson's direction, then looked at Claire again. "He'll be all right till then?"

"I'll redress the wound," Claire said. Swallowing nervously at the sight of his pale face, she shook her head. "Might have to take some more drastic action, too. Listen, other than that, my main concern is those dogs."

"What do you mean?"

"Well, at the minute they're content just knowing we've got nowhere to go but the trees," Claire said. She remembered one night when she was ten or eleven years old and had spoken back to her father for what might have been the very first time. He had screamed the house down as he stormed her into the kitchen, a mountain in the doorway pushing her back against the fridge – and then he had stopped. Sat down on the floor, right there in the doorframe. He hadn't advanced on her after that, but he'd blotted out the only hope of escape. "But they might start getting impatient."

She had sat there for hours, and eventually he had fallen asleep. Only, when she tried to sneak past him into the hall, desperate for a pee—

Sophie nodded. "Right. So you're saying we might need to move on before daylight."

"Fingers crossed, they'll hang on until then," Claire said. She remembered the snatching hand gripping her ankle, her own scream echoing through the house. "But I'd like us to take turns keeping a lookout. "Me and Hudson first. I'll keep him awake, redress that shoulder while we're at it. The rest of you get some sleep, and in a few hours we'll switch."

"You're not counting on us getting a full night's sleep, are you?" Sophie said flatly.

Claire looked out into the sand, her eyes skirting over the seemingly-flat horizon which, in the absence of the torchlight, appeared entirely harmless. "I'd say get an hour or so while you can," she said quietly.

She withdrew her trauma kit from the car as the others grimly rearranged the seats, the sounds of Bugs and Leanne arguing over where to sleep booming faintly through the opened husk of the Landcruiser. Sophie had gone very quiet.

"You okay?" Claire said softly, laying a hand on the young woman's back.

"Yeah," Sophie said, her eyes cold and unblinking. "Yeah, I'm good."

"Get some sleep. It's not your fault," Claire said. She felt faintly nauseous as she realised that she had echoed the words her mother had said to her on that trip to the highlands, nearly thirty years ago now. Claire's father had given up on the car and staggered off to find the nearest pub, and she had spent hours trying to fall asleep on the backseat while her mother sobbed in the front, the side of her face red and throbbing. The sound of the smack still echoed in Claire's ears.

Her father was gone, and she wasn't her mother. Gritting her teeth, she moved around to the side of the car where Hudson was leaning weakly and started to roll up her sleeve. "Million dollar question, kid. You know your blood type?"

Somewhere in the desert, the faint howl of a wild dog echoed into the dark.

The canopy seemed to explode downward, a flood of seething shadow crashing to the floor and bringing a miniature tornado of leaves and broken branch swirling down with it. A cloud of sand sprayed the trees as the titanic weight of the beast punched into the ground. Every particle was a tiny shard of black ichor in the moonlight, many of them spattering the creature's legs and getting lost in the thick, shaggy mess of fur that coated it.

Naomi stared into the enormous mass of oily blackness as it reared up on its hind legs, a ball of dark and mangled shadow lengthening and becoming a shape with stubby arms and a wide, black midsection, its head squat and framed by a mane of dark spines. Its ears were wedges of ragged fur and its eyes glittered darkly. It was the size of a great black bear – bigger, even, towering over them like an elephant – but in shape, it was closer to a koala.

"Shit," Armstrong murmured. He hadn't seen the thing up close before, though he'd seen photographs. It was twice the size he'd imagined, the thin black lips of its bird-like beak peeled back around gruesome blood-stained molars, each one ground down to a sharp ridge.

"Fire!" Joey yelled, swinging his semi-automatic rifle toward the beast. His gloved finger poked blindly at the trigger as he prepared to launch a spray of bullets into the thing's hide—

Too slow.

Naomi cried out in shock as the creature swung an arm in Joey's direction, revealing a portion of its back as its body twisted. There was a flash of black-splattered orange, a quiver of long, sharp spines, then the *smack* of Joey's body crashing into a nearby trunk as the drop bear's claws punched into his stomach and threw him backward.

"Armstrong, get back!" Naomi yelled, but the taller

man ignored her, already storming toward the beast with his rifle raised. The shadows of the trees seemed to twist in on themselves and explode out again as the creature turned, opening its mouth as if to roar. The sound that escaped its throat was a dreadful chirruping, clicking murmur. It leapt on Armstrong before he could react, slamming the tall man into the sand and clamping its jaws around his face.

The rifle dropped from his hand as the trees echoed with the sound of rent flesh and the drop bear ripped all the skin and muscle from Armstrong's skull. It sloughed off wetly and slipped down the creature's bulging throat and Naomi staggered back, her eyes flitting from the creature's bloody face to the convulsing soldier's exposed skull. The enormous creature shot a grin in her direction as it swallowed, raising a set of shining black claws quite deliberately in what looked like a friendly wave before slamming them down into Armstrong's chest.

There was a wet *crack* and the man's body buckled one final time before going still. His ribs caved in and viscera flooded from the cavern of his torso as the drop bear scooped a great handful of twitching red slop out of him and tossed it into the sand.

Somewhere deep in her subconscious, Naomi vaguely registered that it was Armstrong's fading heart.

"Get up, bitch!" Joey yelled, lurching out of the

shadows behind the creature and slamming the butt of his semi-automatic into the back of its skull. The beast whirled around, hardly seeming to note the impact, and grabbed Joey's midsection with two enormous claws.

Naomi watched on helplessly as it started to pull, ripping Joey in two at the stomach. Joey's screams filtered up into the trees as the wet ripping sound of his torso filled Naomi's ears, blood pooling until – finally, with a burst of effortless enjoyment – the drop bear wrenched its paws all the way apart and allowed what remained of Joey to fall to the floor in a wet, slopping heap.

It stood there for a moment, heaving over Joey's spine. Naomi moaned in horror, unable to help herself, and the beast began to turn, facing her with ribbons of flesh still dangling from both its paws. It smiled.

Naomi raised her semi-automatic and the drop bear launched itself forward, batting the weapon out of her hands before she could scream. Immediately her hand went to her belt, fumbling for something clamped there; the drop bear hissed loudly and lurched for her face, ropes of saliva spattering her cheek. "Agh!" she yelled, unsheathing the bulky Glock 17 from her belt and thrusting her arm forward and shoving it into the beast's mouth—

The drop bear bit down and she yowled.

There was a sudden warmth at the end of her arm and she realised that no matter how hard she strained her tendons she couldn't for the life of her squeeze the Glock's trigger. Then she realised the Glock was no longer in her hand – no, the hand was no longer attached to her arm – and she scrambled backward as the drop bear spat both into the sand at her feet in a spray of ichor, its mouth yawing open and that awful half-chirruping half-clicking sound exploding from its throat again.

Naomi looked desperately at the mangled stump below her elbow and tried to scream, hyperventilating in her body armour. God it was going to kill her it was coming and it was angry and hungry and it was going to fucking kill her…

The drop bear wheeled forward with its bloody claws spread, maw open wide, the deep black orbs of its eyes narrow and enraged, nostrils flaring. It was a streak of blood-drenched shadow, a mass of sand rising from the ground and coming for her—

"Fuck!" Naomi yelled, slamming her good hand into the button on her belt. The small device clipped there flashed red, once, and then the drop bear seemed to slam face-first into an invisible wall. It stopped mid-pounce, eyes widening. Lumbering back, it shook its head, great shaggy ears twitching violently as a sound Naomi couldn't hear shot into its skull. The signal was more effective than she could have hoped; as the drop bear stumbled back into the trees, she saw a dribble of blood leaking from its nostril.

The beast shook its head and turned, bolting into the trees in a streak of black and orange.

Panting, Naomi looked in awe down at her messed-up arm and tried not to scream.

Hudson had a little more colour to him, though Claire was reluctant to take her eyes off him for too long. She had redressed his stump with the remaining equipment in the trauma kit but the realisation of exactly what had happened seemed to have begun to settle in him; she saw, more than once, the confusion on his face when he tried to move his arm and found that he couldn't.

Leaning against the car beside him, she looked up into the stars and momentarily closed her eyes. She hadn't been able to take much time to reflect over the course of the day but now time seemed to be stretching endlessly before them, every second longer than the last. The starlit dark was eternal and deafeningly quiet, bristling with the kind of silence that was not the absence of sound, but the heavy presence of something trying not to *make* any.

"So why can't you go to hospital?" she said, turning her head.

Somewhere distant, the long, piercing wail of a hungry dingo echoed across the desert. The sounds had become more frequent, though as of yet the animals had not grown tired of waiting them out. After all,

Sophie's little group had no choice but to go into the trees, and if they tried to make a move in any other direction…

"Hey," she said quietly, nudging him in the side. "Stay with me. Tell me. Why no hospitals?"

Hudson blinked, shaking his head gently. It was evidently becoming more and more difficult for the young man to stay awake. "What?" he started saying, then he seemed to catch up. "Oh. It's complicated."

"So is everything, at the minute." Claire had come to Australia for a fresh start – as far from home as possible, and in one of the only hospitals that would even interview her after what had happened – but she felt less confident about that with every passing second. It felt more like an ending. "You may as well tell me."

Hudson sighed, pinching the bridge of his nose with his good hand. "I… god, I'm woozy, you know?"

"I know. Talk to me. It'll help."

"Talking," he grinned sleepily. "It never really does, does it?"

"Does what?"

"Help. It never helps."

Claire swallowed. She thought about her father, then quickly pushed the thought aside. Unfortunately the only things left to fill the gap that thought left in her head were memories of the weeks and months following her mother's suicide.

Assisted suicide, she remembered bitterly.

Eurydice…

If only she'd told the hospital that she knew the patient in bed eighty-three, then they'd have stopped her from getting involved. But she had wanted to help, in any way she could. Her mother was sick. What they didn't know couldn't hurt them, right?

If only she'd told them, then it would have been some other doctor who'd been faced with her mother's pleading eyes, her weak and coarse voice, her constant begging… it would have been someone else who'd finally pulled the plug on Eurydice and plunged her into oblivion.

"It helps," she said, less surely now, "go on, try it."

It was kindness, she thought. You know what that woman went through. What you both went through. Ending that… it was kind.

"It was kind," she whispered, as if saying it aloud would help it become true.

"What?"

"Nothing. Tell me your secrets," she said, smiling weakly. "Why no hospitals?"

Hudson shrugged – or tried to, then glanced down as if he'd suddenly realised he was outside. "I… well, I just can't. My dad's in the police. When I went m—"

He had stopped, and it took Claire a moment to realise that the silence had been filled in with the distant cries of a small pack of dingoes. They seemed closer than before.

"My parents were crook," he said absent-mindedly after the howls had faded. "I looked up to my dad for most of my life. He was in the police, you know? And I thought… well, I was a kid. I didn't know what the police do to… well, to people like… anyway. I didn't realise he was beating confessions out of innocent people, or stealing cocaine from the evidence locker. Didn't realise how much of the dinner we ate as a family was paid for with bribes and stolen drug money. And then I found out – and I found out my mum was in on it, too…"

Claire swallowed.

"I ran away. I couldn't take it. I think it was the guilt that made my mum drink. But it was the drinking that made her feel even more guilty. And my dad was angry. Brought his work home, let's just say. So I had to go. I'd tried to emancipate a couple years before, but… it's tricky, man. I dunno. I had to run away."

"Yeah," Claire whispered, nodding solemnly. "That's fair enough."

"And I did a real good job, man." He smiled thinly. "Made it look like somebody had taken me, didn't I?"

"Why?"

Hudson tried to shrug again, then shifted uncomfortably, feeling vaguely with his good arm for the missing one. "I couldn't just run; he'd come after me. I'd end up back home, I knew it. But if the police – if my dad – were busy looking for the person who'd *taken* me, then…"

"You could really disappear," Claire said.

"Yeah. Problem is, I made it look too good. I was declared missing within a day, dead within a week. And ever since…"

"Do these guys know all this?" Claire said, nodding to the car behind them. Inside, the faint sounds of snoring rattled the backseat.

"Soph knows. Knows my real name, too. But she wouldn't tell. Anyway, I can't go back. Not to hospital, not anywhere he'd be able to find me. And he *would* find me, before you say anything. He was the one who declared me dead, but I don't think he ever believed any of it. Not completely. And if he realised what I'd done…"

"Yeah."

"I know I'd probably get away with it," he said quietly after a minute. "In and out, no details, no nothing. But I can't… I can't risk it. You with me?"

"Yeah, I'm with you."

"Sophie's been really good to me," he said. "She's a good person."

"I know."

"And I'd follow her anywhere, whatever crazy—"

There was a sudden *paf* from behind the car, the sound of a paw landing heavily in the sand.

Claire lurched upright, beckoning frantically for Hudson to stay put while she fumbled for the flashlight. It wasn't the nature of the sound but the closeness of it, the soft crunch of cool sand under curled claws just a couple dozen feet from the Landcruiser…

Moving around the car, she raised the torch and clicked it on, flooding the desert with a circle of pearly white light.

An enormous dingo stalked slowly toward the car, its head twitching erratically as it moved. Its fur was destroyed and what remained clinging to its gangrenous skin was mangy and matted with blood. Its eyes were shining green discs in the torchlight.

"Shit," Claire said, swinging the torchlight left and right before returning it to the approaching dog. Its ears were large and pointed, its maw a black beacon of sharp bone and teeth. Bubbling white foam drooled over its lips and hung from its jaw in thick blood-streaked ropes.

There was a collar around its neck. Glinting steel buried in the thick mange. But something was broken – it sparked—

"*Shit,*" she said again as the twitching dingo growled in her direction. Its shoulders rippled as it prepared to pounce. Its eyes flashed, and it lurched forward.

9
CONTROL

Sophie Kelly couldn't sleep.

The others had managed, it seemed, and despite everything Leanne, Pia and Bugs almost looked peaceful sprawled across the backseat. The seats had been lowered and they'd found some scrappy blankets to spread across the back half of the Landcruiser; still, it wasn't discomfort that she'd suspected would keep any of them awake. She supposed the exhaustion at this point, coupled with the release of any built-up adrenaline, was enough to counter all the terror.

She doubted any of them would sleep without dreaming.

She sat with her back to the dashboard, watching out of the greasy window as the dark shapes of Claire and Hudson spoke in hushed tones outside the car.

God, she couldn't believe she'd been about to abandon him in the desert just to go after this thing… after all they'd been through?

"You're a fucking monster," she whispered softly to herself. She'd been caught up in it all, so engaged in coming after the thing that had taken everything from her that she'd been prepared to lose everything that she'd built up for herself in the time since. Hudson had been one of the only constants in her life since it had happened… was it worth destroying the thing that had ruined her life, if it meant ruining it all over again?

A sudden flash of light that swung across the windscreen drew her attention to the opposite window and she saw a black shape in the sand, not far from the car. Ears cocked, eyes flaring.

"Fuck me dead," she breathed.

The dingo pounced, flashing across the sand in a streak of black.

"Oh no you don't, cunt," Sophie whispered, lurching forward and slamming open the door.

There was a yowl and a great metallic *smack* as the door smashed the lunging dingo in the face, whacking it off-kilter. The glass of the window shuddered in its frame but held and Sophie's eyes widened in horror as the wild dog wheeled toward her, flashing its teeth.

"Fuck," she hissed, heaving the door shut and scrambling backward.

"What's going on?" Leanne yelled, bolting upright.

Bugs slurred sleepily as Sophie fumbled for the door handle behind her, the dingo slavering at the opposite window.

"Back to sleep, you lot," Sophie snapped, finally finding the handle and snapping the door open. "Mummy's gonna deal with this one."

She rolled out backward like a diver tipping into the sea and her back smacked the sand, much harder than it looked. Before she could make it to her feet the dingo was on top of her, its slobbering jaws swinging great strings of gluey saliva in her face.

"Ah!" she yelled, raising both arms to protect her eyes as the dog bit and snapped, its jaws champing frantically at the air.

A shape barrelled into the dingo's shoulders and Sophie reeled as it was smashed into the side of the car, the Landcruiser rattling with the impact. The shape was Claire; she yelled as she wrapped her body around the creature, her fingers twisted into the wild animal's fur and one of its ears. She wrestled desperately with it for a moment and Sophie was forced to admire the woman's strength, though she didn't dedicate much time to this: instead she scrabbled out of the way and clambered awkwardly to her feet, sand pouring off her clothes in waves. Something moved in the car and she felt eyes watching her from inside; meanwhile the dog had grown tired of the woman clinging to it and it rocked its whole body into the hood, knocking her off.

Claire rolled in the sand and Sophie lunged forward, swiping a sharp, palm-sized chip of rock from the ground. Hudson swayed behind her, his eyes widening as he watched her swing the rock in the direction of the creature's head.

The dingo ducked and snarled at her, its eyes glinting madly as foamy strings billowed from its snout.

"No!" Claire yelled, struggling to her feet as Sophie swung the stone again. "Wait! Look at it!"

Torchlight flared from Claire's hand and Sophie froze as she saw the dingo's face illuminated in that pale white light.

It looked terrified.

The flashing green of its eyes wasn't anger, but desperation; the snarling coming from its throat was more of a pleading mewling sound. "What the…" she whispered, noting its awful mangy fur, the way its body was splayed not in a dominant attack position but one of submission, of fear, its eyes firmly locked on the rock in her hand.

She noticed the thing around its neck and frowned.

"Don't move," Claire whispered, the flashlight clamped between her teeth. Slowly the older woman crept forward, both hands raised before her in surrender. The dingo clocked her out of the corner of its eye and she froze, but when it didn't move to attack she nodded slightly and pressed closer.

"What are you doing?" Hudson hissed. Sophie heard a car door open and shot a look across the top of the Landcruiser, shaking her head in Bugs' direction.

Nobody move.

Gently, Claire reached for the metal ring around the dog's neck. Her fingers trembled. It growled softly at her, then seemed to soften as she found a sort of buckle and unfastened it with a loud *click*.

The collar dropped into the sand and the dingo shook its head, eyes swelling with moisture as it backed up, whole body twitching.

It looked from Sophie to Claire and growled quietly before slinking away.

In moments, it was gone.

"What is that thing?" Sophie said, watching as Claire bent down to retrieve the collar from the ground. It was made of some battered kind of metal, but where small panels had chipped off she saw twisted copper wires intertwining as they ran through it. Tiny bulbs flickered inside the collar, and as Claire ran a hand over the thing she cringed suddenly, dropping it again. "What happened?"

"It… shocked me," Claire said, pinning the torch beam onto the thing.

"It's broken," Sophie said. "The others… d'you think…?"

"Yeah," Claire nodded simply. "Something – someone – is controlling them. Someone used them to herd us toward the trees. They're still out there, surrounding us, but they're not attacking. *Someone* seems to be very patient."

"And this one—"

"Collar broke," Claire said. "It just wanted rid of it."

"Who?" Hudson said, his voice like tar. "Who's controlling them?"

"Someone who wants to keep us out here in the desert," Claire said. "Out here with the monster."

Someone, she noted, observing the faded gecko insignia embossed onto the collar, who knows far more about this thing than any of us.

The inside of the car was cold and the air smelled of stale sweat. Leanne had slept fitfully and for what felt like three minutes in total, and now that she was awake she was acutely aware of just how exposed they were.

Bugs climbed back into the car and forced himself into an uncomfortable sitting position against the back of the passenger seat, leaving the door open so that a faint, warm-ish breeze wafted in after him.

Pia had been sleeping more soundly than the others and was only just waking up, her hair mussed in her face, her eyes red and swollen. Gingerly she eased herself up and the three of them sat there for a minute in silence, a triangle of half-spread legs in the gloomy moonlight.

Outside, Sophie and Claire were talking. Planning.

Leanne wished she'd never come on this dumb trip. If she'd known there was a monster out here she could have at least brought one of her dad's hunting rifles and made herself useful. Oh, that would finally show her brothers. If she managed to drop the drop bear…

"You okay?" Bugs murmured, and she turned her head. She was opening her mouth to lie and say that she was fine when she realised he wasn't talking to her. She closed her mouth again.

"Yeah, I'm fine," Pia said quietly, glancing at Leanne. "How about you two? We haven't had much of a chance to… I dunno. Catch up. Since all this started, I mean."

"We'll have time," Bugs said before Leanne could open her mouth again.

Leanne's stomach twisted a little. She could see blood glittering across Pia's stomach in dark stripes. "Are you sure you're okay?"

Pia looked down, her head swimming. Dark stars danced at the edges of her vision. "Yeah, I'm… yeah, I'm fine."

"Listen," Bugs said, leaning forward a little. "I'm sorry for what I said to you before, Pi. I know that came out a little… forward. I didn't mean to make you uncomfortable."

Leanne rolled her eyes.

"That's fine," Pia said, her voice weak. "Thank you

for apologising."

"I'd like to make it up to you, if I can," he continued. He glanced awkwardly at Leanne before continuing. "Listen, if we get out of here, can I take you for a drink? I'd love to go—"

"Oh, for fuck's sake," Leanne breathed.

Bugs turned his head. "Excuse me?"

"Just leave her alone for ten minutes, would you?" Leanne hissed.

"Why, so you can have her?" he grinned. "Jeez, we all knew you had a thing for *Sammy*, but moving on this fast? That's cold, mate."

Leanne blinked.

Pia's head rolled a little and she frowned in their direction. "What are you two talking about? My head's gone all… swimmy…"

"I can't believe you'd say something like that," Leanne snapped, ignoring her, "you fucking creepy little cunt—"

"Oh, get over it," Bugs spat. "You ain't special, you know, I had just as much of a chance with Sammy as you did."

"Jesus, you're disgusting."

"Guys," Pia murmured. "I think I'm gonna…"

Black clouds blotted out her vision and she rolled forward, tumbling through the open door and out into the sand. The moment she hit the ground she was jolted awake, a sudden pang of agony bolting through her stomach.

"Shit!" Leanne yelled, stumbling out of the car and running around the back to where Pia had fallen. Claire looked up, frowning, and followed her.

Pia lay on her side in the sand, blood spreading slowly through the gauze wrapped around her stomach. Leanne ducked to her side, scooping her head out of the sand. Pia looked up, blinking rapidly, her skin pale in the moonlight.

"We're going to have to go," Claire said, fumbling for the open trauma kit. "Now. She needs more than bandages. You all do. We've stayed out here long enough—"

"You want to go into the trees?" Leanne said.

"It's the only way to Elliott," Sophie said behind Claire's shoulder. "We don't have a choice."

"We can't leave her out here," Claire agreed.

"Okay," Leanne nodded, helping Claire get Pia to her shaky feet. "Okay. Let's do it. It can't be that bad, right?"

A scream came from the trees, perfectly timed to fill the pregnant silence that had been about to drop between them. Claire froze, her blood chilled with terror.

It wasn't a human scream, but the long, wailing squeal of the beast.

10
SEPARATION

The sand bared its teeth behind them as they staggered into the trees.

The moon was a sickly half-disc somewhere vaguely above them, crawling across the starry sky infinitely slowly. Pia was drowsy and her head lolled onto her chest as she was lugged forward. Claire had one side and Sophie the other and one of Pia's arms was hooked across each of their shoulders; their movements, as they stumbled into the shadow of the treeline, were awkward and waddling. As they hobbled with her they left shallow trenches in the sand, burying fallen leaves and fragments of wood.

Beside them Leanne gently guided Hudson forward, her eyes darting from tree to tree in a terrified fervour. Bugs hung back, seemingly stung by something that had happened since Claire had last seen them all; she ignored it, trying to remain focused.

She gazed up into the canopy above them, swallowing at the sight of the dappled layer of silhouette. Despite the fact that there were seldom two trunks within twenty feet of each other, the canopy seemed thick and full, and even where moonlight glittered through gaps in the leaves and branches she could imagine the creature leaping quite easily from tree to tree. Was it up there now, watching them?

"Come on," Sophie grunted, "it's not far through here. We just have to stick to the open spaces, right?"

Claire agreed silently, noting to herself that those open spaces seemed to be growing fewer and further between as they ventured deeper into the trees. In fact, though it could hardly be called a forest – more a collection of sandy clearings with tall, leaning pillar-like protrusions between them – the darkness seemed to duplicate every shadow, thicken every hanging branch, turn the sprouting growths of bush around them into clawed heaps of fingers.

Momentarily Pia seemed to stir from her daze. "Where are we?"

"We're going for help," Leanne said, just a little behind them now. "It's all right, Pi."

Pia nodded, attempting to withdraw her arms from Claire and Sophie's shoulders. "I can walk," she mumbled faintly, but they held on.

"Then walk," Claire said softly. "Lift your feet. But we've got you."

At the back of the group Bugs turned around, walking backward as he looked up into the treetops. They'd seen nothing unusual so far and he was beginning to wonder whether Claire had been wrong about the beast's plans. Surely her whole 'it's heading northeast' thing was just speculation anyway, right? It could have been going anywhere.

But it wasn't like there were many trees around…

Hudson groaned as he stumbled, half-falling onto Leanne. Gingerly the group passed between the trees, sharing skittish looks with each other and with the branches above. The place seemed oddly quiet, stirred only by the ever-shifting moonlight and the soft ground-level bellow of the faintest wind.

Too quiet, Claire thought. That's what somebody would have said in one of those shit horror movies. It's *too* quiet. There was no scuttling of skinks between the trees, no distant warble of a masked owl. Like something had scared them off.

They pressed on, the dark enveloping them.

Claire was about to check if everyone was all right when the canopy creaked above them.

Claire and Sophie froze, Pia hung limply between them. Ten feet or so behind them, Hudson, Leanne and Bugs had stopped as well. Bugs looked up with his good eye while Leanne swallowed nervously, clamping a hand on Hudson's chest to stop him from toppling over.

The sound was like the boughs of a great ship groaning. A confetti of small green leaves fell over them and Claire shook her head. "We have to go…" she whispered, but she couldn't stop herself from looking up into the treetops behind them.

At first she didn't see it. She saw the silhouettes of the branches, and the patches of starlit sky between them that glittered with a careless iridescence. One large patch, she noticed, was entirely pitch black, all the stars within its borders extinguished. Entire universes blotted out.

The patch moved.

Leanne screamed as the beast dropped from the trees into the brush between them. It wasted no time in rearing up onto its hind legs, tilting its head left and right and blinking those awful, dead black eyes. An awful clicking squeal erupted from its throat and boomed into the trees.

"Split up!" Sophie yelled, staggering back and dragging Pia and Claire with her.

The drop bear lurched onto all fours, swinging its body around to screech in Sophie's direction. Its back rippled, a patchwork of bonfire orange and inky jet black, stiff spines trembling across its powerful shoulders.

"We'll find you!" Leanne called back, grabbing

Hudson and heaving him away from the creature's rump. It turned again and roared, its face yawing open, big fluffy ears blown back by the force and heat of its hungry cry. "Bugs, come on!"

Across the clearing into which the drop bear had exploded, Claire and Sophie hurriedly dragged a hobbling Pia between two trees and ducked under a swiping set of claws. "This way!" Sophie yelled, tipping to the right. Claire yelped as the drop bear's fist lashed the air right beside her head.

Then they were running and the others had darted in the opposite direction, the beast scrabbling up into the trees right behind them and following them through the canopy, that great old ship of the woods creaking and groaning all around them as the drop bear hurtled through it.

"It's right above us!" Sophie yelled, looking up despite herself.

"I know!" Claire screamed back. "This way!"

They barrelled aimlessly through the trees, the cracking and creaking following them into the dark as they left the others farther and farther behind. There was no telling where the creature was now – was it right above them? Had it abandoned the chase and gone back for Leanne's splinter group? – and Claire could do nothing but keep running, Pia swinging between the two of them as they lurched forward.

She was running for her life, she realised.

That was new.

Leanne stumbled between two enormous trunks, dragging Hudson by his good arm while Bugs followed behind them. The canopy crackled above them, branches swinging and bending: the wind? Or some kind of hysteric manifestation of the adrenaline surging through her? No, it was coming after them. She was sure…

"Big fuckhead's right behind us," Bugs panted, staggering along beside them. He was out of breath and red-faced, struggling to pass easily between the trees due to the mess of his remaining depth perception. The sand made it hard to run, especially since here it seemed to thinly conceal a layer of hard networked roots and slightly heavier, swampier ground beneath the surface. "I should have gone with Pia…"

Leanne managed to roll her eyes despite everything, ducking under a hanging branch and grabbing Hudson to steer him beneath it. "Can you run?" she said, and he nodded, lurching forward unaided.

The three of them half-stumbled, half-ran through the trees, veering north as the trees to the south thickened. Darkness welled between the trunks in thick and consuming pools of shadow that seemed to reach out with desperate, hungry fingers. The moonlight above them was useless, painting silvery backs upon only the sharpest ridges of each trunk.

Leanne whirled around, stumbling backward with her eyes on the canopy above. There was no movement in the branches, and though it was difficult to hear over the smacking of her heart against her ribcage, she couldn't detect any sound from the treetops.

It had gone after the others.

"Stop," she panted, "stop, both of you…"

They slowed.

Bugs pressed his body against a slender trunk, gasping for breath. His eyes shot up into the canopy. "I can't see it," he wheezed.

Leanne shook her head, looking desperately back the way they'd come. Shit, if it wasn't here then it had gone after Sophie and the others, they were in danger—

"Well, thank fuck for that," Bugs said. He whistled.

"Keep it down," Leanne hissed.

"Oh, don't get sooky with me. We're safe, aren't we?"

"Sophie…" Hudson murmured.

"We have to go back," Leanne shook her head. "Or find another way round. We can't leave them."

"You do you, mate," Bugs said, evidently having forgotten all about Pia. With one final look into the silent treetops above them, he grinned. "It's gone. Fucker."

"Shut up," Leanne snapped. "Just… just fucking

shut up, would you?"

The canopy creaked above them and she froze. They were stood in a small clearing, ringed by a sparse assortment of what looked like slender eucalyptus trees. The three of them formed a triangle of terror in the sand, knotted roots thrusting out of the ground about their feet.

A full minute passed and nothing moved.

"All right," Leanne said calmly, looking from Bugs to Hudson and back again. "It's not after us. If you want to stay here, Bugs, and look after Hudson, then I'm going after the others. If it's come after them, I can—"

"There's no point," he spat. "She was going to leave us, wasn't she?"

"Jesus Christ, mate, that's enough!"

"No," Bugs fumed, stepping into the centre of the clearing. "I've had enough of you pushing me around, cunt. It's not fucking *on*, cunt. And I'll tell you now, if that thing fucking drops out of the trees and snaps you up, I'll be fucking *dancing, cunt*—"

That thing fucking dropped out of the trees.

Bugs screamed.

Naomi Lee staggered into the dark, the Glock gripped in her good hand, ribbons of blood and wasted bone dragging from the grisly stump of the other. She moaned in terror as she ran, her eyes wide and skipping between the trees. The body armour felt less like a protective shell around her ribs and stomach and more a constricting layer of unnecessary weight. She considered removing it – she had seen all the good it did Armstrong and Joey, anyway, and the extra pace she'd gain without the weight would be beneficial – but the time it would take to unclip and shrug it all off was time she didn't have, and besides, maybe it would do *something*.

The wet slopping sound of Joey being pulled apart, Kevlar and all, echoed in her ears.

She could still see the avalanche of bloody organs spilling out of him, the snake-like ruins of his spine slithering down to the ground as his back was wrenched in two.

She was sobbing now, lurching through the trees toward a bank of shadow that she hoped was some kind of exit, some kind of gateway back into the desert. She knew what was out there – *what we* put *out there*, she thought bitterly – but it didn't matter, it was better than this.

She reeled as something moved ahead of her, lunging to one side and ducking behind a tall trunk. Cringing as pain steamed up her arm from the stump below her elbow, she gritted her teeth and waited. Silence for a moment, then a *snap* from behind her.

Closing her eyes, she drew in a sharp, stale breath

and counted to three.

Another *snap*.

"All right, dickhead, the buck stops here!" she yelled, wheeling around the tree and drawing her Glock up in one swift movement.

"Jesus!" Claire wheezed. Beside her Pia's head lolled back as she swung in and out of consciousness. "Put the fucking gun down, Christ!"

Sophie stared wide-eyed at the soldier, eyes scoring invisible gouges in the body armour, the belt, the boots. "What the fuck—"

"The hell are you three doing out here?" Naomi snapped, swinging the pistol from one woman to the other.

"Could say the same for you," Claire said, looking up into the trees. "Where is it? I don't see—"

"You're dead," Naomi said, shaking her head. "I'm sorry, there's nothing I can do for you."

"Well, you could put the fucking gun down," Sophie said.

"Bloody oath to that," Pia murmured sleepily, her arm slipping off Sophie's shoulder.

"Who are you?" Claire said, starting to readjust her grip on Pia's body before realising the girl was trying to stand on her own. Reluctantly she stepped back, only lowering her hands when the younger woman gave her a drowsy thumbs-up. She turned back to the soldier. Her gaze locked onto the barrel of the handgun. "You mind?"

Naomi held the gun steady. "D'you know what you're dealing with?"

"Not a clue," Claire said.

"Drop bear," Pia murmured again.

"That's right. You know it'll kill you?"

Sophie narrowed her eyes. "What *are* you doing out here?"

The Glock swung around, pointed now directly at Sophie's forehead. Naomi had to clamp her teeth together to ignore the pulsing web of agony shooting up her arm, and even then it was like nothing she had ever imagined. The barrel was a deep, black tunnel of death, silent and waiting. "None of your fucking business," she hissed.

"All right," Claire said, raising both hands as she scoured the woman's uniform. "We're not armed. We don't want to hurt you. And like you said, we're all going to die. So put the gun down, yeah?"

There were no insignias, no bars or badges to indicate a rank, in fact no identifying marks at all; the woman's belt was stuffed with empty hoops and there was a slim, softly-flashing device clipped to her waist. The blue light seemed to be one flickering and faintly-ignited bulb of a possible four; the other three were dull and empty: perhaps the device, whatever it was, was recharging.

"I'm a doctor," Claire supplied, glancing down at

the woman's dangling stump. "And I've had some very recent experience with bleeds like that. Let me help."

"Fuck off," Naomi spat, returning the Glock to the older woman's face. Her whole body swayed with pain but she kept the arm steady. Every throbbing heartbeat in her ears was another wall of hot, burning agony smacking her arm and the side of her body. "You shouldn't be out here. There shouldn't be anyone out here. This whole thing's a mess, a fucking mess—"

There was a shriek deep in the trees, a long shrill wail of terror that blasted the shadows around them. It turned Claire's body cold.

"Bugs," Sophie and Pia whispered at once.

11
THE TREES HAVE TEETH

The drop bear filled most of the clearing, an enormous koala-shaped mass of seething black fur with two glaring holes in its face. Its teeth were bared and thick ropes of bloody saliva swung from its bearded jaw as it bore down on him, the exact shape of its body obscured by thick masses of fluffy fur, the spiralling Tartarus pit of its throat a wet, red-raw tunnel that yawed into eternity.

Bugs swallowed his scream and backed up against the nearest tree, splaying his hands desperately at the bark as though he might be able to pull the trunk open and slip inside. The drop bear advanced, its terrible shadow falling over him. It was twenty degrees cooler in the deep shade of the beast and Bugs' blood went ice-cold in his veins, slurring uselessly as his heart tried frantically to pump it harder.

"Cock," he whispered.

"Leave him alone!" Leanne yelled, fumbling for a branch and snapping it off the tree beside her with a hard *crack*. She flung it and the branch struck the drop bear in the back of the neck and bounced off. It didn't turn around, didn't seem to notice.

Bugs shrank back from the thing's face as it took another slow, lumbering step toward him. Its squat, square-ish snout had opened into a vicious smile and he saw flecks of dried blood in its fur, thin streaks of orange and white exploding from its jaw into its cheeks and the thick mass of its beard. Its ears twitched and it clicked its throat.

"Please…" he whispered.

The drop bear roared and a wall of hot air slammed his head back into the tree with a loud, bony report. He whimpered, tears streaming down his face.

"Please…"

The beast grinned.

It ripped forward suddenly, grabbing Bugs' face with both paws and clamping its jaws around his nose. He screamed wetly as it wrenched its head back and spat a clump of flesh into the sand, blood winging from between Bug's eyes. He tipped his head back involuntarily and it dug its teeth into his throat, rending his spine from inside with a sloppy *crunch* and chewing hungrily. A spray of warm red painted the tree behind him and Leanne screamed.

The drop bear tore a chunk of Bugs' neck out and chewed quickly, its molars working to break down the meat in its mouth with a series of loud pops. It punched one clawed fist into the young man's stomach and twisted, unravelling entrails and tipping them out onto the floor. Bugs crumpled to his knees.

"No!" Leanne screamed hoarsely. She felt a hand grab hers and allowed herself to be dragged away, only realising that the hand was Hudson's once they had staggered out of the clearing. "We can't leave him! Please, we can't—"

"He's dead," Hudson growled, hauling her breathlessly forward.

Behind them, Bugs' last scream turned into a thick, hollow gargle and the soft *thwump* of his body hitting the floor filtered into the crunching soundscape of the drop bear feasting on his bones.

"No," Leanne moaned.

"That way," Hudson said bluntly, dragging her toward a gap in the trees.

Leanne's eyes widened as she looked out into the desert. They were so close to the edge of the forest, to escape—

"Look!" she yelled, pointing a trembling finger. Hudson's good arm fell away and he clutched at his wounded stump, trying to get his breath back as he followed her pointing finger with his eyes.

"Oh, bugger me…"

Beyond the trees, the starlit sand stretched out like a flat, grey ocean. It went forever, wave-like dunes crashing on the horizon, clumps of brush and single trees poking up like thorns through leather.

A pack of dingoes paced patiently half a mile from the trees, their eyes flaring in the moonlight.

"No way out…" Leanne muttered, staggering back as she shook her head. "Jesus, what do we do? Hud, what the hell do we do?"

Hudson turned his head to see the drop bear lurching for them through the trees, a mass of hungry black pounding the sand as it roared, strings of flesh and blood ribboning from its teeth.

"I don't know," he whispered, grabbing her hand again. Out in the desert, something howled, and the long, mournful sound triggered a chorus of echoes. "Shit, I don't know."

Bugs' scream pierced the night.

Claire and Sophie shot each other a desperate look, aware now that the drop bear had turned its attention on the others. A silent agreement passed between them: they needed to get back there, and fast, before—

"Get off me!" Pia yelled as the woman with the Glock grabbed her, one-handedly whipping her away from the others and jamming the pistol against her head.

"Aw, shit," Sophie muttered, raising both her hands.

Naomi's brow was hard and her eyes narrow, her face so pale it was almost completely white. Clammy, she said, "Now, listen to me. I'm getting out of here, all right?"

"We're not stopping you," Claire hissed, her own hands raised in submission. "Listen, we all need to get out of here, and you've got a gun. If you could just help us get to our friends—"

"Enough," Naomi hissed, shaking her head as she pushed the gun violently into Pia's temple. "I don't care what you do, I'm getting out of here. Doesn't matter about you or that fucking... that fucking *thing*... I'm out of here, all right?"

She started backward, heading for a gap in the trees. Moonlight filtered into the shadows behind her as she dragged Pia back with her bloody stump wrapped awkwardly around the girl's midsection, her finger twitching on the Glock's trigger.

"No, give her back," Claire said, starting forward then stopping when she saw the desperate wildness in Naomi's eyes. "Please, you don't need her."

"Stay back," Naomi said.

"We're not going to hurt you, for god's sake," Claire snapped. "Give her b—"

Even as she said it, she realised that wasn't why the soldier didn't want them following her out of the trees.

"Yeah, you get it," Naomi whispered. "Keep it busy for me, will you?"

Claire hardened. "You stone-cold bitch."

"We won't come after you," Sophie said, "promise, just – please – she needs help, take her to the hospital at least if you get out of here—"

Claire wheeled around. "What are you doing?"

Sophie shrugged. "She's not going to kill her if we stay back, right? May as well let her go."

"Oh. Yeah, you make a point." Raising her hands again, Claire turned back to the soldier and nodded. "Yeah, take her as far as you can. Just don't kill her. Please."

Somewhere in the woods, the drop bear roared. The guttural rumble boomed into the desert and chilled the night air.

"Fuck this," Naomi whispered, shoving Pia back into the trees and lurching backward.

Claire hurried forward, caught the girl awkwardly and bundled her away from the soldier, her eyes locked on the gun trembling in the woman's hand. "Go," she said. "We're not coming after you."

Naomi swallowed and turned to run. Staggering forward she lurched out of the trees and her boots hit soft sand, no longer run through with the shallow roots of the forest. Turning to leer back at the others, she stumbled out into the crisp, hollow void beyond the trees and whooped.

She had almost made a couple dozen feet when a lithe shape crashed into her from the desert beyond, snapping its mange-covered jaws in her face as a second, sleek mass of shadow leapt onto her chest.

Sophie screamed from the trees as the dingoes ploughed Naomi into the sand at the edge of the woods and burrowed their snouts into the flailing woman's throat and stomach. Her head tipped back and her wide eyes flashed with agony, her lips trying desperately to form a scream that her neck had trapped.

A spurt of blood sprayed Naomi's face as a third dingo slunk forward and buried its jaws in her shoulder, and Claire, Sophie and Pia were left to watch helplessly as the wild dogs dragged her, kicking and screaming, into the desert.

12
SO DO I

The Glock fell uselessly into the sand, a trail of blood smearing the ground as Naomi was dragged screaming away from them.

Sophie's eyes darted to the thing and she lurched forward.

"No!" Claire hissed, barrelling forward to pull her back. For a terrible half-second, the two women stood at the edge of the trees and watched as a small pack of dingoes ripped Naomi's body to shreds. Claire clamped a hand over her mouth and yanked Sophie back from the desert, trying not to moan in horror.

The dogs were savage, their snouts glossy with blood, eyes alight like embers. The sound of it was like pigs slopping at a trough, and the *smell*…

"Help me!" Naomi shrieked, her good hand flailing,

blood-drenched fingers curling and uncurling as she sprawled beneath the feasting animals. The stump of her damaged arm was stuffed deep in the throat of one of the dogs and exploding with spasmodic bursts of crimson. "Help me please god one of youse come and fucking help me—"

The scream turned to a long, wet yawning sound as her jaw was ripped clean out of her skull, teeth, tongue and all.

"The gun," Sophie whispered. It was less than a dozen feet from where they stood, half-buried in the ground with its square, blocky barrel pointed up.

"Not worth it," Claire shook her head. A juvenile dingo, its neck flashing steel-grey where the collar was tightly attached, glanced up at them from Naomi's stomach, ropes of intestine coiled around its snout. It grinned. Its teeth were red.

Sophie nodded. "Let's go find the others," she said quietly, and the darkness closed around them as they turned, grabbed Pia, and staggered back into the trees.

Leanne gripped Hudson's hand and they tore through the woods, his gait odd and unbalanced, her fingers the only thing keeping him upright; they half-tumbled through a clearing and into the dark, thick brush ripping at their ankles.

"It's right behind us!" he yelled, ducking his head

and yanking Leanne with him as a low branch swung into vision. The trees were a blur of streaky white and moonlit grey. He glanced behind his shoulder and saw the drop bear, thundering forward. "Duck!"

He threw his body into the ground; Leanne's hand slipped from his and she rolled away, yelping as her shoulder smashed into a bloodwood trunk and the gashes down her back opened up and beaded with blood.

The beast stood between them and swung its body around to roar in Leanne's direction, its fur streaked with silver in the moonlight. Strings of saliva and blood whirlpooled in the vortex of its throat and Leanne sobbed as she scrambled back in the sand, spinifex scraping the skin of her wrists and peeling layers off her hands. "Leave me alone!" she yelled. "Leave me the fuck alone!"

The drop bear grinned, lurching forward and swiping a paw in her direction. She caught the flash of black, stony claws and tipped back her head, the sharp points missing her neck by inches at most. It raked the air with a second paw, swiping almost blindly at her. It was playing with her, she realised, not taking real shots but toying with her, completely aware that she didn't stand a chance.

"Hey!" Hudson yelled.

The beast turned, its ears twitching as its lips pulled back in a hungry snarl. Leanne struggled to her feet, looking past it in terror as Hudson stood swaying at the other side of the clearing, his good hand bunched into a fist. The stump of the other arm was bleeding again, spots expanding as the compressed bandage strained. His jaw was set, teeth gritted.

"Come on," he whispered.

"*No!*" Leanne yelled as the drop bear leapt, the quivers of its back spreading into a fan of sharp, black needlepoints. "*Hudson!*"

The man lurched to one side and the beast sailed past, smashing into a tree and landing awkwardly in the sand. In less than a second it was on its feet again and snarling in Leanne's direction, but that was enough time for Hudson to sprint across the clearing and grab her, knotting his fingers into her shredded shirt and pulling her to one side just as the giant koala clamped its teeth around the empty air where her face had been.

It wheeled on them as Hudson dragged her between two trees and ploughed forward again, the trunks slamming into its chest so that, for a moment, its great wide head was wedged between them like that of a toddler stuck in the banisters. It roared, that dreadful clicking sound riding the back of a wall of sound unlike anything Leanne had ever heard.

Fuelled by a sudden surge of anger, she roared right back and launched a fist into the beast's nose. Pain ripped through her knuckles in four distinct bolts, her wrist buckling as she followed through into the punch, the drop bear's hard skull barely twitching at the impact.

Leanne's eyes widened as the creature shook its head and grasped both the tree trunks that were holding it back, burrowing its claws into the bark and beginning to wrench them apart with a great groan of wood.

The woods separated and the drop bear flashed its teeth hungrily. There was no hope, Leanne realised as the two of them backed into another tree, momentarily trapped. There was no outrunning it, no fighting it…

The drop bear was inevitable.

The trees seemed to tighten around them as they moved, staggering exhaustedly toward the screaming and deeper into the blood-filled mouth of the woods.

"We shouldn't have split," Sophie panted. "This was dumb. This was so fucking dumb…"

"It's all right," Claire said, equally out of breath. She was tired and only just realising she hadn't eaten since before the flight – what was that, a good twelve hours ago? More? – and that she desperately needed to pee. Funny how things like that slip away from you when you're running for your life from a giant outback terror. "They're fine, they're going to be fine."

"I can't hear Bugs anymore," Pia said, staggering along behind them with one hand pressed to her stomach. "D'you think he's—"

"He's fine," Claire said, "come on, they can't be far…"

She trailed off as they burst into a clearing, a thick crack in the canopy above flooded with silver light. The moon was right above them, a distant and eroded disc of crinkled white like a suspended lamplight. Dawn was still hours away.

There were two bodies in the clearing.

"What the…"

"Oh my god," Pia breathed.

"Same uniform," Claire said, pointing to the nearest. He lay in a mutilated heap, his stomach opened up and spread around him, the scraps of a shredded Kevlar vest the only thing holding his broken chest together. The visor of his helmet had shattered and a spiderweb of cracks shot across his face, broken shards of glass in his open, silently-screaming mouth. "That other woman must have been with them."

"Never mind that," Sophie said, lurching forward and scooping something heavy out of the ground beside the second body. "This is more like it…"

She heaved the thing into her arms and turned, grinning weakly. For the first time since the Landcruiser Claire saw just how exhausted Sophie looked, her arms and face slick with sweat, her eyes propped up by thick red crescents of swollen flesh. Her hair was mussed and smeared with blood and sand, her legs scraped and scratched. Her chest heaved as she gripped the semi-automatic in both hands, wiping it on her shirt to remove some of the soldier's blood. He lay behind her in a pool of fresh, wet blood.

"One for you, too," she said, nodding at an abandoned rifle beside the other body.

Claire glanced at Pia, then nodded. Bending down, she grabbed the weapon and nestled it into her waist, checking it over to see if it was loaded. She had never held one before, let alone fired one, but how hard could it be? Especially when your target was ten feet tall and just as wide. "All right," she said as confidently as possible, looking from Pia to Sophie again. "You good?"

"I'm good. I want it dead," Sophie said bluntly, her eyes like steel.

"Then we'll kill it," Claire nodded.

"You across how these things work?"

"Point and shoot, right?"

"Point and shoot."

"Guys…" Pia whispered.

Claire turned her head and swallowed.

The pointed heads of a dozen dingoes looked back at them from the shadows, low to the ground and growling. Bright eyes flashed impatiently. As Claire watched they slunk forward, filtering to the edges of the clearing.

"I thought they were waiting us out," Sophie said,

coming forward to join them and fumbling with the semi-automatic.

"I think they got bored," Claire whispered. "Or whoever's controlling them did."

"Least we've got these," Sophie said, shouldering the rifle and swallowing as she pointed the barrel into the oncoming pack. There were fifteen or so now, twenty even. More coming from the dark, slipping through the trees like snakes. Angular shoulders twisted and strained as muscular necks turned, snouts twitching in anticipation. Claire saw a tongue lolling in the sand, blood dripping slowly off the teeth that surrounded it.

"We have to go," Claire said weakly, starting to back up across the clearing.

The pack moved as one, eyes blazing. "Shit," Sophie said, looking anxiously from one dog to the next, "they're not gonna—"

"We can't shoot them," Claire hissed. "It's not their fault—"

"We don't have a choice," Sophie snapped as one of the dingoes stepped into the clearing, a large male with ragged clumps of mangy hair for a tail swinging between its powerful hind legs. It growled.

Pia yelped as another came for her, a sleek female with dark patches along her underbelly like scorch marks. Before she could stumble back it had leapt, launching itself into the air in a streak of fiery red. She fell, tumbling to the ground as it slammed into her chest, jaws snapping viciously.

"Christ!" Sophie yelled, swinging the semi-automatic and squeezing the trigger.

The dingo's back exploded into red mist and it squealed, wheeling backward. Claire yelled as the enormous male came forward, baring its teeth then lunging hungrily at her throat. Another report of gunfire boomed around them as she pulled the trigger of her own weapon, punching a string of bullets into the thing's face.

The pack closed in, snarling and darting into the clearing. One snapped at Pia's leg and she reeled, kicking it in the jaw so that its head tipped up, teeth smashing together with a loud clap. Two lurched for Sophie and she staggered back, spraying rounds into them with gritted teeth.

Claire grabbed Pia with one hand and yanked her back as a juvenile pounced in her direction, claws flashing in the moonlight. Another barked savagely as Sophie slammed the butt of her rifle into a third's canid skull, sending it sprawling meekly into the trees.

"There's too many of them!" Claire yelled, whirling around as claws raked her back and sent an ocean of hot, white pain into her ribcage. She squeezed the trigger reluctantly and clipped the wild dog's feet, sending it rolling back toward the edge of the clearing. They were all around them now, dozens of them, snarling and biting, wary of the rifles but hungry enough to champ at the air and swipe furiously.

Another dog landed on Sophie's back and slammed her into the ground. She rolled over and slammed the barrel of her rifle into the dingo's belly, pulling the trigger and screaming as the awful *clap-clap-clap* of the weapon boomed in her ears. The dog buckled and fell of her and another took its place immediately; Claire swung up her rifle and launched another spray into the crowd, glancing about desperately for a way out.

"Come on!" Pia yelled, grabbing Sophie by the hand and pulling her out of the range of two snapping females. Claire followed them across the clearing, firing a quick burst into the sand whenever a dog lunged, surrounded by echoing squeals and savage snarls.

She turned as they tumbled out of the clearing, swinging the rifle left and right. A dingo leapt from the clearing and she shot, cringing at the report and the awful *crunch* of metal striking sharp teeth. The dog fell back and another slunk forward in its place. There were more in the trees around them, slavering madly.

"There's too many," she repeated, almost to herself.

Sophie struggled free of Pia's grip and shook her head, turning to punch another belt of ammunition into the trees. "You two have to go!" she said. "You have to kill it and get the others out of here!"

"We're not leaving you," Claire snapped. "We can deal with this, and then—"

"Shut up," Sophie said. "Listen, I don't know how many rounds this thing holds, or how many we've used already, but…"

She had a point. They could keep shooting, but for how long? Eventually the dingoes would rip them apart before they'd even reached the drop bear. If they could just get to the others…

"I'm not leaving you," Claire shook her head. "Don't be stupid."

"Just listen, I've done my bit, all right?" Sophie said, her back to Claire's, her semi-automatic pointed at a pair of flaring green eyes in the trees a few feet away. She smelled of blood and sweat and her exhaustion seemed to fill the air between them, a thick, depressing haze of heady smoke. "I'm done. If I can get you a few seconds to get out of here—"

"No!" Claire said, anger boiling up inside her. "Listen, you're not doing this! It's dumb, okay? It doesn't fix anything—"

"—says who?—"

"—says me, you fucking idiot! Sophie, d'you know why I'm here? D'you know why I flew halfway around the world? Because I let someone die, back home – I *allowed* them to die, I *helped* them – because I thought it was what they wanted, and I won't do that again!" She was sobbing, she realised, swinging her rifle wildly before her as a dozen sets of bared teeth pushed forward from the dark. All her emotions bubbling to the top and exploding through her as she spoke, a wall of repressed guilt and sorrow finally caving in and its stony remains ripping through her body. "I won't fucking do it again! I couldn't save her, but I can save you, all right? We can get out of here, we can—"

"Stop," Sophie whispered. She turned to catch Claire's eye and smiled weakly. "She was ready to go. That's what she told you, right? Well, who'd be a better judge than her? Claire, it's okay. It's *okay*."

Claire seethed. The anger was nothing compared to the well of grief that had opened in her chest and she shook her head, choking out words through teary eyes. "That's not my point. I can't let you—"

"She wanted to go," Sophie said. All around them, the trees bared their teeth, every opening closed off, pointy-eared shadows slinking through the dark. "So do I."

With that she peeled her back from Claire's and stepped confidently into the trees, whistling as she turned to look back at them. Claire swallowed, her throat hardening as she nodded slightly, an agreement passing between them that couldn't be spoken, shouldn't be.

"Come on, then!" Sophie yelled, pointing the rifle upward and firing a spray of bullets into the canopy. All around them dark shapes growled excitedly, slinking in Sophie's direction as she sunk backward.

"No," Claire whispered, her heart breaking painfully in her chest.

"Kill it, all right?" Sophie called as the mass of dogs closed in on her, becoming less wary of the semi-automatic with every passing second. She fired off another round and the circle widened, just for a moment, then it closed in again. "Kill it for me."

Claire nodded. Eurydice's face passed before her eyes and she sobbed, remembering that expression in the same vibrant, awful detail she always did – but it was different now, the creases around her eyes deeper, their rheumy coating just a little pinker.

She *had* wanted to go.

Claire screamed as the dingoes descended, a great mass of them closing over Sophie. The girl disappeared in the seething crowd, there one moment and gone the next, and before Claire could turn her head away Pia was dragging her by the hand and she could do nothing but watch, horrified, as a whirlwind of teeth and claws ripped into the space where Sophie had stood.

Hudson yelled as the beast ploughed him into the ground, its claws buried in his chest. "No!" Leanne screamed, swinging a branch into the thing's back with a dull *crack*. "Leave him al—"

The drop bear swung an arm and batted Leanne into the nearest tree. The branch fell from her hand as she crashed into the trunk and slid down, head lolling back. Turning its attention back to the boy, the creature opened its jaws and half-squealed, half-screamed, its throat clicking as its enormous ears twitched violently, eyes great black balls of rage. Hudson closed his eyes and wheezed as the claws embedded in his flesh twisted, the weight of the beast crushing his ribs.

There was a great *smack-ak-ak-ak* like thunder caught in a blender and the weight was lifted off him suddenly. Hudson's eyes opened and he looked up to see the beast reeling, viscera unfurling from a wound above its left tufted ear.

"Get up," Claire said, aiming the semi-automatic at the creature with one hand while she reached down to offer Hudson the other. Behind her Pia was wrestling Leanne from the floor.

The drop bear whirled around, blood drizzling into one narrowed eye, nostrils in its beak-like snout flaring as it puffed air angrily. The hole in its head was smaller than it had looked a moment ago, the flow of blood already slowing. Sticky red matted half of the creature's face and drooled off it.

It was even angrier now.

"Get back!" Claire yelled as the thing stormed forward, letting go of Hudson's hand and shoving him behind her. She repositioned the rifle and fired, compressing the trigger for a good two or three seconds. The report of the semi-automatic was enormous, a spray of lead thumping into the beast's stomach and ripping a line of bloody explosions across its midsection. The beast hardly seemed to notice, hurtling toward them now, swinging a titanic arm—

Claire yelped as the creature batted the rifle clean out of her hands, ducking her head as another set of claws winged toward her cheek. As she staggered back the mountain of bloody fur lurched forward, mouth yawing wide, throat erupting into a dreadful roar. Its breath was hot and meaty and ripe, its teeth so close she could see the scraps of flesh caught between them. Its tongue scraped the floor of its mouth like coarse sandpaper as it bellowed, claws splayed like enormous deadly rakes.

"Hey!" Pia yelled, and something small and grey bounced off the creature's forehead. The stone skittered into the sand and the beast turned its head, the roar becoming a vicious snarl. Shoving past Claire the drop bear lurched toward Pia menacingly, its stubby legs shivering as the spiny fur on its back trembled with anger.

"Leave her out of this!" Claire cried, rushing forward and swinging a boot into the back of the monster's colossal knee. It buckled a little, turned its head again—

"Oi! Dickhead!"

The drop bear turned toward the source of the new voice, just in time for the swinging branch Leanne was holding to smash right into its face. It took a staggering step back and another rock pelted its shoulder, powdery sand streaming behind the projectile like a comet trail. "Take that, cunt!" Hudson yelled, already reaching for another rock.

Claire grinned as the creature stepped back again, glancing around before lunging for the nearest tree. Pia ducked her head as the thing bounded up the trunk and into the canopy above them. Right above their heads it turned, clinging to the branches with one arm, its legs wrapped around the trunk. Claws flashing, it roared again, chunks of spittle flying from its mouth.

Claire's smile faded.

"Run," she whispered.

Dingoes howled in the distance as the four of them carved a ragged path through the trees, a thick dark mass of shadow moving in the canopy above. The drop bear snarled and panted as it followed them, swinging between branches and leaping where the gaps between trees widened. The trunks croaked and groaned under its weight, bowing and cracking at the roots.

"There!" Claire pointed, chest heaving, legs aching like hell. Ahead of them the trees opened up onto the wide, flat sandscape of the desert, but she wasn't pointing at the sand. There was something out there, something black and glinting in the moonlight—

Hudson screamed behind her as the beast dropped from the canopy, folding him into its paws and ripping a great hunk out of his stomach with its teeth. "No!" Pia yelled, starting to turn, but Claire grabbed her shoulder and hauled her back, flailing and kicking.

"There's nothing we can do," she whispered hoarsely. Leanne shrieked as the colossal koala punched its sharpened molars into Hudson's neck and ripped it open, spraying blood and flecks of cartilage.

"I'm sorry, but we have to go!"

Hudson crumpled and the beast turned its head, blood swinging from its mouth and coating both paws with glossy, shining red. It grinned and lunged after them.

"Now!" Claire yelled, shoving Pia ahead of her and reaching back to grab Leanne's hand. The two of them ran, legs pumping hard, the sand beneath their feet becoming softer as they neared the edge of the trees.

Leanne's hand slipped from hers as they barrelled out into the desert. "Is that—"

"Must be!" Claire yelled, grabbing her again and hurtling for the thing, a squarish monolith of polished black metal and glass in the sand. The Jeep was parked at an angle, a colossal four-wheel-drive that looked brand-new in comparison to the battered Landcruiser they'd come here in. It was painted jet-black; Claire could only assume that this was the vehicle in which the three soldiers had arrived. "Get in!"

Pia had already staggered to the passenger side door of the Jeep and she wrestled frantically with the handle, her hands sweaty and slick with blood. Out in the sand dozens of pairs of flashing green eyes moved like swirling stars, predator dogs slinking closer in the dark.

There was a *crunch* and the drop bear swung out of the trees behind them, landing on all fours in the sand. A great cloud of blood-red blossomed about its paws as it bounded forward.

"Come on!" Claire yelled, then she cried out in agony as sharp claws raked her thigh. Stumbling forward she wrapped her arm around the handle of the driver's side door and yanked it open, folding her body into the car just as the drop bear slashed at her again. A single claw caught her cheek and drew a lightning-hot arc of blood into her mouth. Beside her Pia slammed her own door shut as Leanne clambered into the back, almost rolling over herself. "Shut the door!"

The third door slammed and the beast slammed its body into the side of the car, rocking the whole thing like a wrecking ball smashed into a hatchback.

"Did they leave the keys?" Leanne panted, grabbing both headrests and searching the footwell frantically as if she might find another pair of semi-automatics down there.

Claire fumbled behind the wheel and relief flooded her chest as her fingers found the keys, jammed into the ignition. "Lucky day," she whispered, turning them as the drop bear slammed into the car again—

The engine sputtered, whined, and died.

Claire's heart stopped for a moment. Desperately she tried the ignition again; the car protested, a dreadful clicking wheeze erupting from beneath the bonnet. "No!" she yelled, looking up to see the giant koala grinning at her in the wing mirror. "No, come on, come on…"

On her third try the engine coughed to life.

"Yes!" she screamed, slamming it into gear – just as the drop bear leapt onto the roof, an enormous cone of splintered metal appearing in the ceiling. Leanne yelped, ducking her head as she scrambled half into the footwell. The drop bear slammed a paw into the metal and another, smaller cone appeared, right above Pia.

Claire swallowed. Forget first gear, she thought, slamming the knob into reverse and hammering down the accelerator. There was a mechanical scream as the engine protested and the Jeep shuddered backward. Above them the drop bear bellowed, sliding off the roof and jouncing into the sand.

"Hit it!" Pia yelled, gripping a grey leather handhold and shrinking into the passenger seat. Claire gaped through the windscreen as the drop bear rose to its hind legs, somehow seemingly twice the size as it had been before. Chest heaving, great clawed arms hanging by its ankles, it glared back at the car and flashed its teeth. "For Christ's sake hit it now!"

Claire pumped the car into gear and slammed her foot down. They rocked forward, the engine keening awfully as they carved great raw trenches in the sand beneath them. "Hold on!" she yelled.

There was a metallic *crunch* as they smashed into the drop bear's stomach and ploughed it backward, a sudden bolt of inertia slamming Claire's head into the wheel. Blood spilled into her eyes and she ground her heel into the pedal, the tyres spinning as they fought against the titanic weight of the beast and rammed it back into the trees. She was screaming, she realised, not in pain but in adrenaline-fuelled anger, putting every ounce of strength she had into the accelerator until she heard the drop bear's back *snap* and the tree it had been smashed against lean back into the woods—

Quickly she shifted gears and spun the Jeep away, the drop bear falling onto its stomach in the sand. It wasn't down for long; as the big black four-wheel-drive hurtled into the desert it rose up in the rearview mirror, a mountain of orange and black and violent rage.

"Shit," she said, eyes flickering up into the mirror as it started thumping after them, taking great bouncing strides across the sand. She ploughed them through an ocean of flashing green eyes, the wild dogs keening back as the Jeep thundered into the middle of the pack.

Her phone was buzzing in her pocket. She fumbled for it as she drove, leading the drop bear out of the trees and into the dark, her head swimming. The phone bounced out of her hands and into the passenger footwell.

"Pia," she panted, "grab that, would you? That's Dr Franklin."

Pia swiped the phone and stared at her in shock. Behind them the drop bear was gaining, thundering across the desert and swiping away dingoes as they advanced, pawing limp bodies into the dark like they weighed nothing. "This is not the time to rearrange your interview!"

"It's not that!" Claire yelled, swinging the Jeep to the right as a bank of pointy-eared shapes rose up before them. It couldn't be, not at this time of night. "It's about Brody!"

"The cryptozoologist," Leanne muttered in the backseat. "What—"

"Just answer it!" Claire yelled.

Pia raised the phone to her ear, clutching at her stomach with her free hand as she looked up into the rearview. The beast had changed course and couldn't be more than thirty feet behind them now – twenty-five – twenty—

"Hello?" she called into the phone, then listened as Dr Franklin spoke hurriedly, his voice crackling through the speaker.

There was a splintering *crunch* and a scream of shattered glass as the drop bear leapt onto the back of the car and bellowed, shoving its face in through the exploded rear window.

"I'll call you back!" Pia yelled.

"Well?" Claire said, yanking the wheel down hard and turning them a hundred-eighty degrees in the sand. Vertigo swelled in her swimming head and she looked up to see the drop bear still attached, clinging to the back of the car like a leech, its jaws snapping wildly as it champed at the back seat.

"He says Brody was poisoned!" Pia yelled. "He's in a coma – Claire, he said he did some digging, managed to trace the poison back to some chemical company in Melbourne—"

Leanne screamed as the beast thrust a paw into the car and swiped at her face, ducking further into the footwell behind Claire's seat. "Fuck me!" she yelled, trying to reel in her splayed legs as the monster clawed and bit at her. "Does this thing go any—"

There was something down here with her and Leanne grabbed it, hoping to throw it into the creature's face. Her fingers wrapped around the leathery folds of a thick black utility belt and she glanced down, finding a small device in her sweaty palm.

"What the—"

Claire swung the car around and the drop bear squealed, still latched onto the back of the car. "What is it?" she shouted over the scream of the engine. The Jeep smashed into a pair of snarling dingoes and batted them into the sand.

Leanne shook her head. The device was the size of a walkie-talkie but with only one button and a row of tiny, unlit LED bulbs. "It's just a little… thingy," she yelled back. "It's a button. It's useless!"

Claire's eyes widened as she remembered the device she'd seen clipped to the female soldier's belt.

"It might not be!" she called. "Press it!"

"But it's just a—"

"*Press it!*"

Leanne slammed her thumb onto the button and the drop bear shrieked, its whole body convulsing as it withdrew from the back of the car and tumbled into the sand. The device flashed brightly but there was no sound, nothing they could hear anyway—

Claire spun the car around and slammed on the brakes, saw the drop bear flailing in the sand a little way ahead of them. Its claws were clamped down hard over its tufted ears, its mouth open and screeching, eyes wide with agony.

"It's a signal," she whispered.

Her jaw set and she slammed her foot down on the accelerator, the Jeep lurching forward at her command. They covered the distance in less than a second and there was an almighty crash as they slammed into the drop bear, launching it onto its back. Pia screamed beside her as she heaved the wheel to one side and braked again.

The engine died. "Keep your finger on that button," Claire whispered, fumbling for the doorhandle and wrenching it open.

She staggered out into the sand and around to the back of the Jeep, her heart hurting, her back and leg and face burning where the thing had clawed her. Please, she thought, wrestling the trunk open, please, for the love of *something*…

The trunk was crammed with guns.

"Oh, thank you," she whispered, her hand trembling as she reached inside.

Claire stumbled drunkenly to the spot where the drop bear lay, cowering with its paws over its ears. A mountain of horror and violence, curled up before her in the foetal position.

Trembling, she raised the Glock 17 and pointed it at the creature's face.

The signal was doing something awful to the beast, making all its spiny hairs stand on end like it had been shocked. Its whole body quivered and convulsed erratically. For a moment she almost felt sorry for it.

Bloody, breathless, done, she squeezed the trigger.

The gun fell from her hand and she staggered back, chest heaving, the mania pumping through her blood finally spent. Turning her head, she yelled, "You can turn it off now!"

Silence fell, absolute silence, and she realised that the ground beneath had been vibrating slightly. The drop bear lay dead and broken behind her, its face a wreck of bloody ribbons, its body limp and still.

Panting, Claire started toward the car.

Done.

It was done.

Flaring eyes watched her from the dark but hung back, seemingly wary of her.

"I need a nap," she whispered as she stumbled for the Jeep. "Jesus. Oh, Jesus, I need..."

The ground was vibrating again.

She froze as a faintly familiar sound rang out behind her, turning slowly to see a faint cone of light growing in the dark. Something coming. Something in the sky...

"What the shit..."

The sound became a soft thumping then a faint *thwub-thwub-thwub* and then, as the ball of light in the air grew brighter and closer still, she realised what she was looking at.

"Oh, fuck me..." she whispered, suddenly wishing she hadn't dropped the gun.

"What is it?" Leanne called from inside the car.

Claire's eyes widened. "Drive," she yelled, backing away from the thing as it dropped suddenly, the ball of light becoming a floodlamp that consumed her, encircling her and the Jeep in a blinding halo of white. *"Pia, drive!"*

The helicopter shuddered toward them and she watched its belly open, dark silhouettes appearing in the cavernous opening of its stomach. Soldiers, half a dozen of them. The blades whipped around and a cloud of sand bloomed like a miniature sandstorm beneath the vehicle, obscuring her vision.

Not before she'd seen it though. The logo on the side of the helicopter, painted on oily black with faint, graveyard grey…

A sprawling gecko, eating its own tail.

"Hands up, back against the car!" somebody yelled through a loudspeaker, their squawking voice booming into the desert. Long snaking trails of black swung out of the helicopter as a wall of heat billowed into her and Claire realised they were ladders. "Get your hands above your fucking head and step away from the koala!"

"Oh, shit," she whispered.

BOOK TWO
EMU WARS
COMING SOON

READ ON...

BONUS PREVIEW
CHAPTER
OVERLEAF!

PROLOGUE
BRODY

The door to Brody's ward swung silently open, a wedge of pale fluorescent light dropping unceremoniously onto the floor where it stretched and yawed into a trapezium of lurid white. He turned his head away from the window with some effort, his neck and chest aching. Outside the baked red vista of the desert was sandwiched between a flat grey slice of hospital parking lot and the endless, cloudless dome of the sky.

"The nurse told me you were awake," Dr. Franklin said, stepping onto the ward and closing the door quietly behind him. There was no need to be so cautious – everybody in the room, save for himself and Brody, was in a coma – but still, he had always felt uneasy speaking too loudly in the proximity of so many sleeping patients. After all, they might be able to hear him, somewhere in there. Somewhere in the subconscious. That made him wholly uncomfortable.

"You're Australian," Brody murmured, his voice thick with the medication pumping into him. He was sixty-four years old, with a shock of white hair usually fixed into a passable combover but right now splayed on the pillow behind him, thin and damp with sweat. "I made it off the plane, then."

"Just about," Franklin said, pulling up a chair beside Brody's bed and checking the machines. They beeped quietly as he scribbled notes. "You had an attack in the air. Luckily for you, there was a medical doctor on board – Claire Casey, her name was – she saved your life."

He leaned back in the chair and tucked the notebook into his pocket. He wore the white coat with a loose shirt and suspenders underneath, a pair of round glasses balanced on his nose. His hair was dark, but might have been dyed; the roots were a different colour altogether. He was thin and square-jawed, his body lean and comfortably folded around itself in the chair.

"Funny enough, she was meant to interview here when she landed," Franklin said. "Disappeared, though, right after sending you my way. Gave me a call and asked me to check in on you. You must've made an impression."

Brody shook his head wearily. He felt groggy, his

chest weak and throbbing, his limbs numb and hanging uselessly by his side. His head pounded. "How long was I out?"

"You've been asleep for a couple days," Franklin said. "Not too long, considering. Listen, is there anybody I need to call? Family, friends? Someone you were coming to meet? Anyone that could come and—"

Brody's eyes snapped wide suddenly. He lurched forward in the bed, grabbing Franklin's coat with a hand that felt thick-fingered and tingled with pins and needles. "Sophie," he said breathlessly. "Oh, god. A couple of days? Christ, she's in danger. Sophie Kelly. Is she here?"

Franklin took Brody's hand and eased it from his lapel. He shook his head. "Nobody's asked for you with that name. Is Sophie family?"

"She asked me to come out here. To help. With the creature…"

Franklin frowned, pushing his glasses up his nose. "I don't know what you—"

"The bear," Brody hissed. "The drop bear. It came after her and her friends, they needed me…"

"You're not making any sense, man."

"The creature. The drop bear—"

"The drop bear isn't real," Franklin insisted. "It's a myth, made to scare off tourists and kids. I don't know what you've been told, Mr. Brody, but if somebody's playing a trick—"

"They're all in danger," Brody hissed desperately. He moved awkwardly, trying to swing his legs over the edge of the bed. Immediately Franklin lunged, taking the old man by the shoulders and easing him back into bed. The monitor by the bedside beeped more insistently than before. Was that his heartbeat? Why did it smell so strongly of disinfectant in here? "They need me. You don't understand, doctor. I'm a cryptozoologist – I *know* it's real – I was asked out here to help them…"

"Maybe," Franklin said quietly, tugging the bedsheets tightly over Brody's legs before returning to his chair. "But then you had your attack. Listen, the woman who sent you here, Claire, she called me to say she couldn't make her interview, that she was in a difficult situation. It sounded like there were people around her, young people. Is it possible that whoever lured you out here with this… this *drop bear* nonsense could have lured her too, in your place? That whatever they needed from you, they got from her instead?"

"Nonsense," Brody scoffed. "I have seen things you wouldn't believe, doctor. Things you couldn't begin to imagine. You think a giant koala is too out-there to be real? Your mind is closed to the possibility of—"

Franklin raised a hand. "You need to remain calm, Mr. Brody. You've just woken up from a minor coma after a very traumatic physical event. You need to rest, d'you understand this? Listen, if there's anybody we can call, you let me know. Otherwise, I came in here to check in on you and to pass on some information."

"What information?" Brody said, his mad white eyebrows furrowing into a frown as he turned his head.

Franklin sighed. "Listen, your heart attack wasn't entirely… natural. Casey asked me to keep an eye on you – though I'm not completely sure why – and implied there might have been something suspicious about the attack. Now, I've seen your bloods, Mr. Brody, and this may come as a surprise, but it looks like you were—"

"Poisoned," Brody finished.

"Yes…" Franklin blinked. "Yes, poisoned. Listen, I can't say I haven't been somewhat intrigued by this whole situation."

He leaned forward, reaching into his coat, and produced a piece of paper that he unfolded as he spoke.

"I did some digging. I shan't bore you with the details, but I managed to trace the poison back to a pharmaceutical company in Melbourne – I doubt you will have heard of them. Whatever's going on here, drop bears or not… somebody didn't want you to make it off that plane, Mr. Brody."

He handed over the paper and Brody looked, his mouth open a little, the throbbing in his head growing and growing in intensity. On the paper was a grainy, awkwardly-formatted printout of a single image, with a single word beneath:

G.E.C.K.O.

The image was a logo, presumably the logo for the pharmaceutical company Franklin was talking about. A crisp, green image of a gecko, its blobby fingers latched onto some unseen surface. Its tail was impossibly long and looped into a circle, the point burrowing into the creature's mouth like the little green lizard was eating itself.

"*Gecko*," Brody whispered. "Who are you?"

A NOTE FROM THE AUTHOR

Thank you for reading *Drop Bear*. As an independent author every single person reading my work is so valued and I can't express how much your time means to me. For more of my books, follow me on Instagram @heath_horrorwriter or check out my website derekheathhorror.com where I'll keep you updated on future releases.

I hope you enjoyed! If so, please leave a review on Amazon if you can. I'd love to know what you thought.

www.ingramcontent.com/pod-product-compliance
Lightning Source LLC
Chambersburg PA
CBHW031241210726
48287CB00003B/850